## FLIRTIN' WITH DEATH

Black eyes blazing, Long Shadow stormed up to Reese and snarled, "You disgusting slime! You put your filthy mouth on my wife and you hit my son! Nobody touches my family, Curry! Nobody!

"Nobody, eh? Well, I just did, lawman. There ain't no law on the books that says I can't kiss a squaw or smack a redskin brat, is there, Marshal? I mean, you can't arrest me for those kinds of pleasures, can you?"

Long Shadow's muscular chest heaved with suppressed rage. Gritting his teeth, he breathed hotly, "So you really want a fight that bad, eh?"

Narrowing his eyes, the thick-bodied man laughed maliciously and replied, "Yeah, I sure do."

"Well, you are getting your wish," Long Shadow responded, taking off his badge. Turning to Frank Denton, he handed him the shiny six-pointed star and said, "I'm taking a brief leave of absence. Barry is officially marshal until I put this badge back on. What I'm about to do will be as a private citizen—husband of my wife and father of my son."

Eyes shining eagerly, Reese stepped to the center of the street and shouted, "Come on, Indian yellow-belly. Let's get on with it!"

Long Shadow stepped momentarily to April Dawn and said, "I'm going to fix him so he won't be able to kiss anybody for a long time. . . ."

**The Badge Series**
Ask your bookseller for the books you have missed

THE BADGE: BOOK 21

★

# DEADLOCK

★

## Bill Reno

Created by the producers of
**The Holts: An American Dynasty,
Stagecoach,** and **White Indian.**

*Book Creations Inc., Canaan, NY • Lyle Kenyon Engel, Founder*

BANTAM BOOKS
NEW YORK • TORONTO • LONDON • SYDNEY • AUCKLAND

DEADLOCK

A Bantam Domain Book / published by arrangement with
Book Creations, Inc.

Bantam edition / February 1991

Produced by Book Creations, Inc.
Lyle Kenyon Engel, Founder

DOMAIN and the portrayal of a boxed "d"
are trademarks of Bantam Books, a division of
Bantam Doubleday Dell Publishing Group, Inc.

ISBN 0-553-28849-0

Published simultaneously in the United States and Canada

Bantam Books are published by Bantam Books, a division of
Bantam Doubleday Dell Publishing Group, Inc. Its trademark,
consisting of the words "Bantam Books" and the portrayal of a
rooster, is Registered in U.S. Patent and Trademark Office and in
other countries. Marca Registrada. Bantam Books, 666 Fifth Avenue,
New York, New York 10103.

PRINTED IN THE UNITED STATES OF AMERICA

OPM     0 9 8 7 6 5 4 3 2 1

# DEADLOCK

# ★ BADGE ★

**G**raceful, surefooted, and gloriously free, wild horses once thundered across hills, valleys, and mountains of the Old West by the thousands, an embodiment of the ideals of that time and place. Today their number has diminished, with one of the largest American concentrations at the Pryor Mountain Wild Horse Range on the Montana-Wyoming border. Once caught, the animals are quickly domesticated, especially if surrounded by tame horses. This increased their appeal to Indians and ranchers looking to increase their wealth or to prevent the feral creatures from interfering with their livestock. Sadly, it also contributed to their decline.

## ❖ BADGE 21: DEADLOCK ❖

# Chapter One

The late morning wind blew eastward across the Wyoming border into South Dakota that early May day in 1894, and the warm sun proclaimed that summer was fast approaching the grassy hills. Two scruffy-looking riders coming from the east topped a gentle rise and pulled their mounts into the shade of a stand of cottonwoods and willows, then drew rein. Their arrival stirred the blackbirds resting in the trees, sending hundreds of them squawking and flitting into the clear blue sky.

The riders' hats were weather-beaten, their boots were scuffed, their Levi's were dirty, and their sweat-stained shirts looked as if they had not been removed in months. When they pulled off their hats to sleeve the sweat from their brows, their long, greasy hair was revealed, and it was evident it had been at least a week since they had put a razor to their faces.

The men stared westward at the rooftops of Cheyenne Crossing, South Dakota. Walt Frick, a burly man of forty, spit a brown stream of tobacco juice into the lush green grass and dismounted, gesturing with his jaw toward the town. "You can't miss him, Harry," he said to his partner. "He's a purebred Cheyenne with skin as dark as old mahogany, and he's about six-five, slender, and rawboned. With his boots on, he seems as

1

tall as one of these cottonwoods. That's why they call him Long Shadow."

Harry Denker, a small, waspish runt of a man, dismounted as well and studied the blunt, seamed face of his friend. Finally he said nervously, "Just 'cause I ain't never seen him it don't mean I never heard about him. Why don't you just forget it, Walt? I'm afraid you'll get yourself killed."

"I didn't ask your advice. I just want you to find out where he is," the big, ugly man snapped. "You come back here with that information, and I'll take it from there."

Worry showed on the smaller man's face. "But that Indian is greased lightnin' with his gun. I've heard all kinds of stories. You're flirtin' with death."

Fury leapt into Frick's wide-set eyes, and his words were venomous. "That rotten Indian lawman put me behind bars seven years ago, and every livelong day, while I was languishin' in that stinkin' prison, all I could think about was gettin' even with that scum! Then at night I dreamed about it! Every miserable day for seven long years I itched to kill that towerin' totem pole—and now it's time to scratch that itch!"

Frick paused to catch his breath, then said, "I'd go into town myself, but there'd probably be people who'd remember me. If they did, they'd holler for Long Shadow, and my chance to square things would be gone. As it is, the only way I'll get him is to shoot him in the back. No man yet has drawn against him and lived to tell the story."

Frowning, the little man pressed, "You're sure you want to back-shoot him?"

Matching the frown, Frick responded, "Whaddya mean?"

"Well, when you shoot a man for revenge, it ain't as

satisfyin' unless you can see his face when you shoot him."

Frick spit another brown stream and chuckled. "Don't you worry none about that, Harry. Sure, I'd like to face him head-on and let him see who was killin' him. I'd like to tell him how much I hate his stinkin' guts just before I send him into eternity, but I'll have to forgo that particular pleasure in order to make sure of killin' him and walkin' away in one piece. I can handle it. The main thing is I want to see that scummy redskin dead."

Denker grinned, revealing his yellow teeth, and nodded silently. He then turned and mounted his horse, and looking down at his friend from the saddle he promised, "Okay, Walt. I'll locate the redskin for you. When you see me comin', you'll need to hurry into town and sneak into position, so's he don't have a chance to go off after I learn where he is."

"I'll be ready," Frick replied. "You just be ready to hightail it outta these parts as soon as I cut him down."

"I'll be hangin' around close, ol' pal," Denker promised. "I want to watch you get him." With that, the little man trotted his animal toward town.

Frick spit out the entire plug of tobacco, then pulled a fresh supply from a shirt pocket and bit off a corner. Content, he sat down on the grass and leaned his back against a tree, watching Denker until he disappeared from view at the edge of Cheyenne Crossing.

Harry Denker kept his horse at a steady trot as he headed for town. He knew a man from Cheyenne Crossing who now lived in Sioux Falls, and it was from him that Denker had learned so much about Marshal Long Shadow. He decided that if anyone asked why he was inquiring about the lawman's whereabouts, he would simply say he had stopped to greet Long Shadow for their mutual friend.

Denker rode onto Main Street, assessing the town. Several blocks of homes surrounded the business district, which was five blocks long and lined with false-fronted clapboard buildings, some freshly painted and others showing the wear of sun, wind, rain, and snow. Main Street was fairly crowded, with people milling about and various vehicles and riders moving in both directions.

Riding the length of the sun-drenched street, looking for the marshal's office, Denker passed three saloons—the Pine Tree, the Rusty Lantern, and the Broken Spur. Finally, in the middle of the fourth block, he spotted the marshal's office and jail, which unlike the town's other buildings was made of stone and looked quite formidable.

Dismounting at the hitch rail, Denker stepped onto the boardwalk—allowing two women to pass—and reached for the knob on the door of the marshal's office. He twisted it, but nothing happened. The door was locked. Cursing under his breath, he was just turning away when a tall, slender man dressed in a suit and string tie came out.

Denker was startled at first, remembering that the marshal was tall and slender, but he saw quickly that the well-dressed man was not an Indian and wore no gun or badge.

"Looking for the marshal?" the man asked with a smile.

"Uh . . . yeah," Denker answered, scratching his bristly chin. "You happen to know where he is, mister?"

"Doctor," the man corrected in a noticeable English accent. "Dr. Ronald Tottingham. And you are . . . ?"

"Uh . . . Harry Denker," the outlaw replied quickly. "From Sioux Falls."

"Welcome to Cheyenne Crossing," the doctor said. "I don't know the marshal's whereabouts, but I can take you to the man who does. Come with me."

Tottingham led Denker next door to the Black Hills Gun Shop. Halting at the door, the physician explained, "Barry Hawkins, our gunsmith, serves as deputy marshal whenever Marshal Long Shadow is away. So he'll know where he is."

Entering the shop, the men found thirty-three-year-old Barry Hawkins busy at the workbench, repairing a broken rifle stock. The doctor introduced Denker to the gunsmith, then asked, "Do you know where the marshal is, Barry? Mr. Denker wanted to see him."

Hawkins smiled and nodded. "He's gone deer hunting across the Wyoming border in the direction of Sundance, but he should be back by sundown. Is there something I can do for you, Mr. Denker?"

"Not really," Denker replied, scratching his wiry beard again. "I just stopped by to greet the marshal for a mutual friend who used to live here. He lives in Sioux Falls now, and he's spoken often of the marshal. Too bad I missed him, but I'm just passin' through and I gotta keep movin'. Thanks, anyhow."

"Who is this mutual friend?" Hawkins asked. "Maybe he's somebody I know."

"Frank Webb," came the response.

"Must have been before my time," Hawkins mused. "The name's not familiar."

"Then it is certainly before my time," Tottingham said with a chuckle. "You've been here longer than I have."

"Well, thanks, gentlemen," Denker stated, heading for the door. " 'Preciate your time."

Minutes later he galloped back toward Walt Frick, and he saw Frick mount up quickly at his approach. Drawing to a halt, the smaller outlaw said, "No need to hurry, Walt. The marshal ain't in town."

"Where is he?" Frick demanded, scowling.

"Went deer huntin'."

"Did you find out where?"

"Yep. His deputy told me Long Shadow's huntin' across the Wyomin' border in the direction of Sundance and he's expected back by sundown."

The burly man cast an eye toward the sun and said, "It's not quite noon. If we head out right now, we'll have time to search for him before he heads back for town. And it'd be easier gettin' away after killin' him if we can catch him in the hills." Frick paused, then asked, "Did he go huntin' alone?"

Shrugging his narrow shoulders, Denker replied, "I don't know. I didn't think to ask."

"Oh, well, if there's somebody with him, it'll just be too bad for him, too." His face was grim and determined as he added, "Ain't nobody gonna get in the way of me havin' my pound of flesh."

Spurring their mounts, Frick and Denker rode northwest toward Sundance, Wyoming.

Marshal Long Shadow moved stealthily through the dense timber in the rugged Black Hills country shared by South Dakota and Wyoming, and the wind that sent sparse, cottony clouds scudding across the blue sky high above the forest rustled the branches of the juniper, pine, and paper birch trees. The air was clean and clear, and periodically the lawman looked over at the flat pinnacle of Devil's Tower to the northwest, picturing in his mind the Belle Fourche River wending its way snakelike past the base of the tower in its journey southward.

The tall, slender, full-blooded Cheyenne paused and removed the bone-white Stetson from his head. Running a sleeve of his fringed buckskin shirt across his moist brow, Long Shadow looked down at his nine-year-old son standing beside him. The boy's bright gaze locked with his father's, and a smile spread across his dark face. The tall man smiled back and said, "You think you're a man now, eh, Little Sun?"

Little Sun idolized his father, and his garb—boots, Levi's, shirt, and hat—was exactly the same, except that no badge was pinned to the front of his shirt. He also did not wear a Colt .45 strapped to his waist, but for the first time he was allowed to carry a rifle on a hunting excursion with his father. The boy had owned the Remington .44-caliber bolt-action rifle for nearly two years and had been trained by Long Shadow in its use, but he had only shot at bottles and tin cans. Little Sun had often accompanied his father on hunting trips to observe, but now Long Shadow was completely satisfied with his son's marksmanship and was ready to see him make his first kill as a hunter. They had been stalking a huge buck deer for over an hour, and the magnificent animal was slowly working its way to higher terrain, unaware that the hunters were on its trail.

Responding to his father's words, the lad smiled and said, "Carrying my rifle doesn't make me a man, Papa. It's how I use it that will show if I'm now a man."

"You are showing wisdom," Long Shadow remarked softly. "And you are most certainly on your way to becoming a man."

Side by side, father and son continued to track the deer, stopping periodically to scan the rugged land ahead of them. They halted beside a stream, and Long

Shadow knelt down and was scooping up water and drinking when Little Sun pointed through a break in the trees. "Papa, look!" he exclaimed in an excited whisper. "There he is!"

Rising, Long Shadow followed the boy's finger and smiled. The buck was some five hundred yards ahead and above them, slowly turning its antlered head and sniffing the wind.

"You have good eyes, Little Sun!" the lawman whispered back. "You're going to be a great hunter!"

The buck turned and meandered into the deep shadows of the timber. Long Shadow said, "We mustn't get too far from the horses, son. We'll return to them and bring them higher."

"But Papa," the boy protested, "the buck will get away from us if we take the time to go after the horses."

Laying a firm hand on Little Sun's shoulder, Long Shadow replied, "You must learn the patience of the hunter as well as the persistence. It isn't good to stray too far from your horse. The buck is in no hurry. We'll catch up to him if we're patient. But you must remember that in this rugged country that is sometimes hostile to men, it is always possible to get hurt or injured. If such a thing were to happen, the closeness of a man's horse could mean the difference between life and death. Do you understand?"

"I understand," Little Sun replied, nodding.

"All right," the towering lawman said with a smile. "We'll hurry to our horses and soon be back to track down the buck, adding persistence to patience."

As father and son moved back through the forest to their horses, they talked of many things, and soon the boy guided the conversation to his Indian heritage. Long Shadow was pleased that as the boy matured, his interest in his forebears was increasing, and lately he asked more and more questions about his people, the Cheyenne.

Reaching the horses, the lad said, "Papa, tell me again how you became an outcast from the Cheyenne nation, and how you ended up as a lawman in a white man's town."

Long Shadow chuckled, shaking his head. "You've heard the story so many times. You really want to hear it again?"

"Yes, I do," Little Sun replied flatly.

Mounting up, with the packhorse following on a lead rope, they headed back toward the spot where they had last seen the big buck. As they rode, Long Shadow recounted the story of how, at fourteen, he had almost been hanged by a group of angry white men who thought he had stolen their horses. Cheyenne Crossing's marshal at that time was a stocky, muscular widower named Boyd Dollar. The marshal had come along just as the white men were cinching the rope on the youth's neck and stopped the lynching, saving Long Shadow's life. A short while later, Cheyenne warriors captured Marshal Dollar and were going to torture him to death in retaliation after Dollar killed two Cheyenne braves in self-defense.

Long Shadow had pleaded with his chief, the venerable Black Thunder, not to kill the man who had saved his life. But the chief believed that Dollar had shot down his two braves by stealth and refused to listen to the youth's pleas; he was determined to put to death—as slowly and painfully as possible—the man responsible for the deaths of his warriors. Long Shadow was unable to accept such injustice, and while a pit of coals was being prepared for the torture, the young Indian had managed to set the lawman free.

"And that's why my grandfather cast you out of the Cheyenne nation, wasn't it, Papa?" Little Sun interjected.

"Yes." Long Shadow's eyes seemed slightly unfocused, as if he were seeing the past. "Even though your mother was only thirteen and I was but fourteen, we loved each other very much, and she summoned the courage to beg her father to reconsider his action. Black Thunder would not listen. I can still see the fury in his eyes and hear the scorn in his voice as he called me a traitor and banished me from the Cheyenne nation forever."

Little Sun studied his father's face. "That must have hurt you very deeply, Papa."

"More than I could ever describe," Long Shadow replied softly. "So, as you know, I became an outcast from my people, and your grandfather ordered me never to try to see his daughter again." He smiled, adding, "But I did. My love for your beautiful mother was too great, and I could not stay away from her. On a few occasions, I risked my life to creep into the village and see her."

Little Sun asked, "It was right after you were sent away from your people that Marshal Boyd Dollar adopted you as his son, wasn't it?"

"That's correct," Long Shadow replied. "I have many fond and wonderful memories of the man I called Dad. As a matter of fact, I idolized him so much that I wanted to be a lawman just like him. He wasn't particularly fond of the idea and tried to discourage me, pointing out that I would have an especially hard time pinning on a badge because I am an Indian. As you know, white men are not always fond of us."

The boy sighed. "Yes, sir."

"Anyway, it took a long time, but I finally showed the people of Cheyenne Crossing that I could be a good lawman. When Dad was killed in the line of duty in 1883, the people made me their marshal."

"They sure like you now, don't they, Papa?" asked the boy with a grin.

"Well, they seem to," Long Shadow concurred, chuckling.

Little Sun bent over his saddle to avoid a low-hanging tree limb, then noted, "I guess the person who liked you the most back then was Aunt Sally, right, Papa? You almost married her."

"I did, but that's because I thought your mama was dead. In 1877 the Army moved all the Northern Cheyenne to Oklahoma. Two years after that they were moved again, to the reservation in Montana where they still are today. I rode out to meet them when I heard they were coming through near here, but your uncles, Leaning Bear and Soaring Eagle, told me that your mama had died. It was a lie, but I didn't know it. The truth was April Dawn had remained behind in Oklahoma, to be with your ailing grandfather. After he died, she was forced to stay there another five years before the Army took her to her people."

The boy's face was solemn. "Mama told me that you had rescued Aunt Sally when she had been abducted and mistreated by the two renegade braves Marshal Dollar later killed."

"That's right. Over the years Sally and I became close friends, and when I was told that your mother was dead, Sally confessed that she loved me and would become my wife if I would have her. Although I was still in love with the memory of your mother and knew I always would be, I was lonely and wanted to have a family. Then, the day before our wedding, your mother came to Cheyenne Crossing—and knowing the love that your mother and I had for each other, Sally stepped aside and let us have our happiness."

"Aunt Sally is a wonderful person, Papa," Little Sun said with conviction.

"That she is, son," Long Shadow agreed. "That's why we consider her far more than a good friend; she's part of our family—which is why we think of her as your aunt. I'm very glad that she's found love and happiness with Ronald Tottingham. She certainly deserves it." After a brief pause, the tall lawman grinned and said, "I'm glad for something else, too."

"What's that, Papa?" the boy asked.

Leaning from his saddle, Long Shadow clamped a strong hand on Little Sun's shoulder and answered, "I'm very glad that almost exactly a year after your mother and I were married, you were born into our family."

The handsome lad patted his father's hand and said, "I'm quite happy about that myself."

The two laughed together, and then the boy said, "And you named me Little Sun because the sun and a shadow are very closely related, as are the sun and the dawn."

"That's right," Long Shadow confirmed, smiling. "The perfect name for the son of April Dawn and Long Shadow. And then—"

"Yes, I know," Little Sun cut in with a tone of mock sarcasm. "Then when my sister came along four years later, you named her Star Light because the stars occupy the same sky as the sun."

"Exactly. And even though you like to pretend that you are burdened with a sister, I know you really love her with all your heart."

Bowing his head, Little Sun peered up at his father and grinned. Then his eyes widened and he pointed.

The buck was standing on a rocky ledge three hundred yards away and about fifty feet higher. The Indians reined in and quickly dismounted, leading the horses into deep shade. Rifles in hand, they moved quietly toward the deer.

The midafternoon sun threw slanted rays through the forest as father and son drew near the big buck. Hiding behind two pine trees about twenty yards from the deer, they assessed the situation. The magnificent animal was standing in an open area, facing them, and Long Shadow whispered, "This is your moment, my son. If you shoot straight, you'll become a blooded hunter. Aim for his heart."

Little Sun's own heart was drumming against his ribs. Licking his lips, he kept his eyes on the buck while he quietly worked the bolt-action lever and jacked a cartridge into the chamber. Then he carefully shouldered the weapon, drew a bead on the deer, and pulled the trigger, shattering the silence of the forest with the sharp crack of the rifle.

The high-velocity slug plowed into the great buck's heart, killing it instantly. As the echo of the rifle's report clattered across the hills, the animal collapsed onto its belly, its knees buckling. Reflex caused the buck to jerk twice, then roll onto its side.

Elated, Little Sun raised his rifle and screamed a wild cry of victory.

"You did it!" Long Shadow shouted. "You hit him square in the heart! Come, my son. You must now be anointed."

The Indians hurried to the dead buck. Almost reverently, the boy fell to his knees beside the carcass, his hand trembling as he touched the soft fur at the rib cage that minutes earlier had heaved with breath. Slowly he ran his hand down the chest, holding his fingers less

than an inch from where the .44-caliber slug had pierced
the hide and exploded the heart.

The Cheyenne lad was awestruck. By his own nerve
and skill he had taken the deer's life so that his
parents and sister would have food. Long Shadow knelt
beside the boy and murmured, "This is a sacred moment to our people, Little Sun." As he spoke, he pressed
his forefinger into the bloody wound; then, the tip of
his finger glistening with blood, he made a vertical
streak on each of the boy's cheeks.

His eyes misty, the proud father said, "You have now
been blooded, Little Sun. You are a hunter."

The boy blinked away his own tears as he stood up.
Looking down at his father, who was still on his knees,
he whispered hoarsely, "Am I now a man, Papa?"

Long Shadow rose, towering over the lad, and rested
a hand on his shoulder. "A lot of growing must take
place in your body and in your mind, my son," he
answered softly, "but in your heart and in your spirit
you are now a man. I am very proud of you."

Laying his rifle on the ground, Little Sun wrapped
his arms around his father's slender waist and embraced
him for a long moment. When the boy let go, Long
Shadow said, "You wait here with your kill. I'll go get
the horses."

# Chapter Two

**W**alt Frick and Harry Denker worked their way through the dense Black Hills forest, trying to pick up Marshal Long Shadow's sign and getting increasingly disgusted because so far they had not been successful. Frick spit brown tobacco juice as he halted his horse beside a small brook and said, "I don't know, Harry. We might have to go on back to town and wait for that stinkin' redskin to show up. It's like lookin' for a needle in a haystack out here."

"Maybe he went on into Sundance," Denker suggested, hauling up beside Frick.

While their tired horses drank from the stream, the bigger outlaw replied, "I guess he could have. Let's have some water, too, then take a ride over there and see."

Both men dismounted and were bellied down on the bank, drinking, when the crack of a rifle reverberated across the forest. The outlaws' heads came up, and they looked at each other, eyes wide. Leaping to his feet, Frick pointed due north. "It came from that direction! Let's go!"

Tying their horses to some nearby bushes, the two men threaded their way through the trees, climbing higher as they ran. After a few minutes they reached a rocky ledge and stopped to catch their breath. The land took a dip in front of them, and off to their right was an open meadow. Suddenly Frick elbowed his friend and whispered, "Harry, there he is!"

They quickly squatted down, then made their way to a stand of junipers. Hunkering in the shade, they looked into the distance and watched Long Shadow cross the meadow, his rifle in hand, heading for the forest. Neither the Indians' horses nor Little Sun were visible from the outlaws' vantage point, and they presumed the lawman was alone.

"Looks like he's gonna be comin' straight at us, Walt," Denker declared. "Let's intercept him."

"Yeah, come on!" the big man responded eagerly. Running from tree to tree, he led Denker toward the oncoming Cheyenne. Stopping momentarily behind a stand of brush, Frick pulled his revolver and said quietly, "We'll get the drop on him and disarm him. Then we'll tie him to a tree so's I can have me some fun before he dies."

"You gonna torture him?"

"I guess you could call it that. I'm gonna beat him to a bloody pulp; then I'll shoot him."

Denker chuckled with anticipation.

After a few more minutes of weaving through the forest, the husky Frick abruptly jumped behind an outcropping of rock, motioning for his partner to follow. "We gotta be careful, now," the big outlaw warned. "Let's wait here, since it's just off the path. As soon as he passes, we'll come up behind him and give him one heck of a surprise."

Striding rapidly across the grassy meadow, Long Shadow was anxious to get the deer loaded on the packhorse as quickly as possible. April Dawn always worried if he was late getting home from hunting, and he made it a practice to be back before sundown. Reaching the dark shadows of the trees, he had just passed a rock formation and was about to turn and head for the horses when a sharp voice cut the air.

"Hold it right there, red man!"

The voice was directly behind him, and the marshal knew by the tone that he was in trouble. Halting instantly, he turned slowly and found himself looking into the muzzles of two revolvers. The faces of the men holding the weapons were slightly obscured by the shadows, made even deeper by their hats. Long Shadow's body was as tight as wire as he demanded, "Who are you, and what do you want?"

"You'll figure it out soon enough," came Walt Frick's cold voice. "Right now I want you to drop that rifle; then ease the revolver out of the holster and let it fall. Make a quick move and you're dead."

Long Shadow had heard the voice before, but he could not place it. Knowing he had no choice but to obey—he might be able to draw and fire his revolver fast enough to take out one of them, but not both—he let the rifle fall to the ground, then slowly removed the revolver with the tips of his fingers and dropped it next to the rifle.

"Okay," Frick said, motioning toward a birch, "stand against that tree."

As they shifted position, sunlight fell on the outlaws' faces. When Long Shadow got a good look at the burly man's features, his mouth pulled into a thin line.

Frick guffawed. "See there! It didn't take you long to recognize me, did it? And you know what I want, don't you? I want your stinkin' red hide!"

Feeling completely vulnerable without his sidearm, Long Shadow glared at the outlaw with his black eyes. His voice level and steely, he stated, "You'd better forget whatever you have in mind, Frick. You'll be sorry if you don't."

Walt Frick threw his head back and laughed heartily. Elbowing his partner, who stood close, he said, "You hear that, Harry? I'm the one holdin' the gun, and he's givin' *me* the warnin'."

Denker grinned broadly and shook his head. "That does beat all, don't it?"

Frick's laughter suddenly died. His face went almost purple as he bared his teeth and growled, "I'm gonna have my revenge, tin star!"

Little Sun sat beside his kill for some time until, finally getting restless, he stood and looked around. Moving aimlessly, he kicked a few stones and finally decided to see if his father was returning with the horses. He hurried to the crest of the meadow, then stopped and looked down into the forest, in the direction Long Shadow would be taking. Abruptly, his mouth fell open in fright. Two men were tying his father to a large birch near the edge of the timber.

His heart leapt to his throat. Ducking, he peered at the scene, wondering who the men were and why they were doing that to his father. More importantly, he wondered how he was going to help Long Shadow, for he was certain the men meant to do him harm.

Suddenly something Little Sun had never felt before came over him. His flesh tingled and a strange fire kindled in his breast. Pivoting, the boy dashed to his rifle, which was lying beside the dead deer, and levered a cartridge into the chamber, then started back across the meadow. He kept to the shadows as he entered the forest and slowly worked his way down toward the three men.

*        *        *

Cold sweat beaded on Long Shadow;s brow. Harry Denker held him at gunpoint while Walt Frick lashed him to the tree, binding his wrists securely behin the trunk. Finishing the knot with a grunt, the thick-bodied outlaw stood inches from Long Shadow's face and spit tobacco juice into his eyes. The Indian blinked against the burning fluid, but said nothing. Laughing, Frick batted the hat from Long Shadow's head, then slapped his cheek hard.

The outlaw's eyes blazed as a dark flush crept over his ugly face, and his breath was hot as he rasped, "I've waited seven years for this, Indian scum! Seven long years!"

"You put yourself in prison, Frick," Long Shadow responded evenly. "Don't blame me for it."

"It was you who arrested me!" Frick countered. "It was you who put me in prison!"

"I was just doing my duty as a lawman."

"Your duty!" The stout man spat. "You mean the duty that comes with this cheap piece of tin?" As he spoke Frick snatched the badge from Long Shadow's shirt and threw it over his shoulder.

Denker giggled, picked up the badge, and pinned it on his own chest. "Lookee, Walt! I'm a lawman now!"

Eyeing Long Shadow with disdain, Frick remarked, "Yeah, he don't look so tough anymore. Seems like we dehorned the big bull!" Stepping close to the marshal, Frick laughed gleefully. "You know what I'm gonna do, red scum? I'm gonna punch you in your ugly, dark face once for every month I spent in that rat hole. But don't worry, I won't knock you out. This'll be done real slow-like, so you can feel every one of the blows good and clear. And when you're a bloody mess, I'm gonna kill you. What do you think of that, lawman?"

"You're playing with fire, Frick," Long Shadow responded. "You kill me and there'll be a dozen badges breathing down your slimy neck."

Mockingly, Frick trembled all over. "Oh-h-h! This big tough marshal is scarin' me to death!" His face hardened as he continued. "The only time I was really scared was when I was in prison. I was scared I might catch pneumonia or somethin' like that and die before I got out. Then I couldn't catch up to you and kill you! But I got you in my hands now—and you're gonna pay!"

Planting his feet, the burly outlaw drove a violent blow to Long Shadow's midsection. The Indian doubled over as breath gushed from his lungs. Grinning, Frick said, "That was just to soften you up a bit before the *real* punishment begins!"

With that, he planted his feet again and drew back his right fist, shouting, "This is for the first month, red scum!" The fist cracked against Long Shadow's jaw, whipping his head to the side. Then Frick's left fist slammed him savagely. "That's for the second month!" the outlaw breathed, taking a step back.

Blood trickled from the corner of Long Shadow's mouth. Looking slightly dazed, he shook his head, straining against the ropes that bound his wrists behind the tree.

Denker giggled once more and quipped, "I don't think he likes what you're doin' to him, Walt. He don't look none too happy."

His hands on his hips, Frick guffawed. "He ain't gonna like it any better as time moves on, neither!"

The outlaw was about to strike Long Shadow once more when a high-pitched voice cried, "Don't you touch him again, mister! Untie him!"

Long Shadow's head whipped around, and he looked past Frick. Little Sun was standing there, his face fiercely determined, holding his rifle on the outlaw.

Frick wheeled around and eyed the small boy with

contempt. Denker tensed, obviously waiting to see what his partner was going to do.

Little Sun was trembling inside, but he refused to let it show. "Untie him!" he commanded a second time.

Frick winked at Denker, then said to the boy, "Well, I do declare! We got us some more red scum! From the looks of him, I'd say he must be a chip off this old block. This your old man, kid?"

"He is my father," the nine-year-old corrected, feeling the butterflies that fluttered against the walls of his stomach. "Untie him."

"Tell you what, kid," Frick said with a sneer. "You'd best put that there gun down before you get hurt."

"It's not pointed at me, mister," Little Sun said tightly. "It's pointed at you."

The hefty man laughed scornfully. "Now, you ain't gonna shoot me, red runt. Put down the gun before I lose my temper."

Turning to Long Shadow, Frick said, "If you don't want to see the brat get hurt real bad, you'd better tell him to do as I say, Marshal."

"He knows how to handle the rifle, Frick," Long Shadow warned. "You'd better do as *he* says."

"He ain't gonna shoot me!" the outlaw scoffed and smashed Long Shadow on the jaw.

Little Sun knew he had to show he meant business. Lining the rifle muzzle on Frick's left shoulder, he pressed the trigger and the rifle barked. The big man screamed and went down. Working the lever like a veteran, the boy swung the gun on Denker just as he was pulling his revolver. Little Sun had no choice. If he did not shoot the smaller outlaw, the man would shoot him. The split second that he had did not allow time to plan a crippling shot. The boy fired point-blank, and Denker flopped flat to the ground, the slug through his heart.

Little Sun jacked another cartridge into the chamber and swung the muzzle on Walt Frick, who was lying on the ground, moaning and trying to get his revolver out of its holster.

"Don't move, mister!" the boy shouted. "I'll shoot you again!"

Gritting his teeth with pain, Frick looked into the boy's eyes, and it was obvious that he knew Little Sun meant what he said. The outlaw took his hand away from the gun and used it to squeeze his bleeding shoulder as his gaze shifted to the lifeless body of his partner.

Long Shadow looked at his boy with pride. "Little Sun, you did well," he murmured. "Take the man's gun from his holster and throw it out of his reach—and keep your rifle pointed directly at him while you do it. Don't take your eyes off him. If he so much as flinches, shoot him."

The boy nodded, then followed his father's instructions.

"Good," Long Shadow breathed. "Now, come and untie me."

Frick lay on the ground, watching intently while Little Sun freed his father. When Long Shadow stood over him, he gasped, "You gotta get me to a doctor, Marshal. I'm bleedin' like a stuck pig."

"I have no obligation to do anything for you," Long Shadow snapped.

"Yes, you do!" Frick bawled. "You're a lawman! You have to! You can't let me bleed to death!"

Long Shadow stepped to Denker's body and retrieved his badge. After pinning it back in place, he removed Denker's shirt to use as a bandage for Frick's wounded shoulder, and as he knelt beside the outlaw, he growled, "Unfortunately, you're right. I can't let you bleed to death, Frick . . . as much as I would like to. I have to take you in for trial for assaulting an officer of the law with intent to kill. But, on the bright side, those charges will send you back to prison for a long, long time."

Frick's already pale face lost more color.

"Where are your horses?" Long Shadow asked him.

"About . . . about three hundred yards straight south."

Turning to Little Sun, Long Shadow said, "Go get them. We'll take the other man's body to town for burial and this man to the Tottinghams'."

The boy nodded and wheeled to go, but his father's call halted him in his tracks. Long Shadow's face reflected his pride and his concern. "It makes me sad that you had to kill a man today, my son, but I commend you for your quick thinking and good shooting. If you hadn't acted as quickly as you did, they would have killed us both."

The boy held his father's gaze for a long moment, smiled at him, then headed down the slope for the outlaws' horses.

As soon as the deer was tied to the packhorse and Harry Denker's body was draped over the back of his own mount, the lawman hoisted Walt Frick onto his saddle. Riding side by side, the marshal and his son led the other horses out of the forest, back to town.

At his ranch some four miles north of Cheyenne Crossing, elderly Clarence Potter was working on the water pump when three riders rounded the side of the house and came toward him. Recognizing the three Curry brothers, Potter stiffened with anger, and a flush rose under his shirt collar, for he knew what they had come for.

Elvie Potter—who at seventy-six was a year younger than her husband and quite frail from a weak heart— was in the kitchen when she heard the hoofbeats in the yard. Stepping to the open window, she parted the curtain and looked out. At the sight of the men, she began to tremble. Leaning against the sash, she breathed, "Dear Lord, why do there have to be people like the Currys in this world?"

Bud, Jake, and Reese Curry were twenty-nine, twenty-six, and twenty-four, respectively. Bud was the tallest of the three, and though he was quite muscular, he was slender. He and his youngest brother, Emmett, who was twenty, were the best-looking members of the family and resembled each other strongly. By contrast, Jake and Reese, like their fifty-four-year-old father, Abner, were of average height and stocky—and also like him their features were blunt and ugly.

As the threesome came closer, the rancher felt anger as well as fear, not knowing to what lengths they or their father would go to try to force him to sell his ranch to them. Whatever they were up to, Potter was determined not to bend. He and Elvie were too old to pack up and move elsewhere.

The old man trembled inwardly as the men dismounted. Releasing the pump handle, he nervously wiped his hand on his pants. As water from the spout dripped noisily into the nearly full water trough, Clarence forced his voice to remain steady as he said, "I know what you're here for, and you're wasting your time. You may as well get back on your horses and ride."

The three men encircled the rancher, glaring at him coldly. Bud said, "Now, just a minute, Mr. Potter. You ain't heard our offer."

"I don't need to," Clarence retorted. "The place isn't for sale."

Reese positioned his bulky body close behind the old man. "Just listen to the offer, Mr. Potter," he urged. "I'm sure you'll change your mind."

Clarence turned to look at him and said, "You heard me. The place isn't for sale."

His face darkening, Reese swung an elbow, thumping Clarence on the shoulder, and the impact would have knocked the old man down had Reese not reached out and gripped the rancher's arm. Icy sweat formed on Clarence's brow beneath the brim of his tattered old hat as Reese squeezed hard on his thin arm and hissed, "You gonna listen to the offer?"

Clarence did not answer, but he looked back at Bud.

"I think he's ready to listen now," spoke up Jake, who stood opposite Reese.

Grinning wolfishly, Bud asked, "How many acres you got here, Mr. Potter? 'Bout sixty?"

"Fifty-five," Clarence answered, his tone flat.

Bud frowned and rubbed his chin. "Only fifty-five, eh? Well, I'll tell you what. My pa told me to come and offer you eighteen hundred for the place, thinkin' there was at least sixty acres . . . but I'll stick my neck out and offer you the same amount even though there's only fifty-five. Now, how's that for generous? Your house and buildings are in pretty shabby shape, so I'd say you'd be plenty foolish not to sell."

Clarence lifted his hat and wiped away the sweat from his forehead with the back of his hand. Fearful, but determined to turn them away, he replied, "Your offer is *not* generous, and you know it. My house and outbuildings are in good repair, and you know that, too. This ranch is worth no less than four thousand dollars—but even if you offered me *ten* thousand, I wouldn't take it. Like I told you, the place isn't for sale. This is our home—and has been since Elvie and I came here over forty years ago. We raised our children on this place, and we're going to live here the rest of our lives."

Without warning, Reese slammed the old man with his shoulder, knocking him down. Leaning over, he tightened his fingers around the rancher's belt and jerked him to his feet. Shaking him savagely, he blared, "You better take the offer, you old duffer! If you don't—"

"Leave him alone!" Elvie Potter suddenly railed.

Clarence looked toward the porch where his wife now stood, her right hand pressed against a post for support. Breathing hard, he called, "Please go back in the house, honey."

"Not until these crooks leave!" she replied, glaring heatedly at all three.

"We ain't leavin' till we've come to an agreement on the sale of this run-down old ranch!" Reese bellowed.

Struggling against the hand that held him, the old man countered, "We're not coming to any agreement! Now, let go of me!"

A sound of fury erupted from Reese's throat as he abruptly jerked Clarence toward the water trough and forced him down to his knees. While Elvie's screams echoed in the yard, Reese plunged the old man's head into the water and held it there. Clarence struggled and writhed against the muscular man's powerful hands, but to no avail. Finally, when he began weakening, Reese brought him up.

As the rancher gasped and coughed, his wife left the porch and stumbled toward the trough. "Stop it!" she shrieked. "Leave him alone!"

Reese stepped in front of her, blocking her way. When she stopped and looked up at him with a mixture of terror and anger in her eyes, he commanded, "Go back in the house, Mrs. Potter. This negotiatin' is for us menfolk." When Elvie hesitated, he roared, "Go back in the house, lady, or you'll be next in the water trough!"

The old woman's trembling hand went to her mouth,

and she slowly began backing away. After a few steps, she turned and shuffled to the house, breathing with a labored wheeze and clutching her chest. Reaching the porch, she stumbled up the single step and dropped onto a wooden chair.

Shaking Clarence hard, Reese demanded, "You ready to do business, old man?"

"I told you," Clarence choked, "this place is not for sale."

Cursing, the husky man rammed the rancher head-first into the water again, holding him under for a long time, while his brothers looked on without emotion. When Reese pulled the old man up, he shook him violently, blaring, "You want some more, Potter? Now, my brother made you a liberal offer for your ranch. Just say we got a deal, and everything will be okay."

The old man's thin gray hair was matted to his head, and water was dripping down his face. His lip quivered as he answered, "We can't sell to you. We're too old to make a move. Elvie couldn't take it. She isn't well. Tell your pa not to send you over here anymore. This ranch is not for sale."

Blood pumped into Reese Curry's cheeks. Clenching his teeth, he plunged the rancher's head into the water once more, holding him there for better than a minute. Clarence thrashed and kicked, but he could not free himself. Finally Reese pulled Clarence's head out of the water and let him fall to the ground, where he lay gasping for breath and spewing water.

Waiting till the oldster had stopped sputtering and rolled onto his hands and knees, Reese stood over him and growled, "You and your wife better think it over. If you don't sell us the place, some kind of 'accident' could happen." Bending down so that his face was inches from the old man's, he snarled, "What I'm sayin' is that the two of you just might end up buried on this place sooner than you planned—a lot sooner."

The rancher's eyes filled with fury and he snapped, "They hang people for murder!"

"Who said anything about murder?" Reese retorted slyly. "An accident ain't murder."

"Get off my property! And don't show your face again, or you'll have Marshal Long Shadow to deal with!"

Reese's face went even darker at the mention of the marshal. His eyes narrowing, he warned, "You've got a couple days to think over our offer, and you'd better give it some real serious consideration. And if you say anything to that redskin marshal—or anyone else—about this visit, your lovin' wife just might end up with a couple of broken arms. You got that?"

The old man shifted his gaze to Elvie, whose face was as white as chalk as she sat clutching her chest. Clarence looked back into Reese Curry's malicious eyes and replied softly, "We won't tell anybody."

"Good!" Reese declared triumphantly as he straightened. Nodding toward his brothers, he said, "Remember, we'll be back to see you in a couple days."

The Currys mounted up and rode out of the yard toward the road. Their business uppermost in their minds, the brothers were barely aware of the three riders coming down the road toward the ranch, leading a horse with a dead man draped over the saddle and a packhorse with a dead deer tied to its back.

Reese commented, "Ain't a doubt in my mind they'll accept our offer. Just like the other ranchers we've, uh, *persuaded* to sell, they'll see the wisdom of it."

"Yeah," Jake agreed. "And just like the others, they're too scared to go runnin' to that stupid marshal."

"Speakin' of the devil," Bud remarked, suddenly fo-

cusing on the oncoming procession, "that's him in the
lead up there. See? You can tell it's him, and he's got
his kid with him."

Reese squinted at the riders. "Yep, you're right. And
I'd say by the way that fella behind is leanin' over his
saddle horn, he's got a bullet in him. The other one
looks deader'n a doornail."

"We're gonna reach the gate just about the time they
pass it, Bud," Jake said nervously. "What'll we do?"

"Just ignore him," replied the elder brother. "And if
he looks to be suspicious, or asks any questions, I'll do
the talkin'."

The sun was low in the western sky as the marshal,
his son, and their prisoner approached the gate of the
Clarence Potter ranch. Seeing the Curry brothers, Long
Shadow felt his body stiffen, and he hoped they could
continue on their way without an encounter. He threw
a quick glance at his son, who eyed him in return with a
look of concern on his face. No one in the valley liked
the Curry family, and their reputation was well de-
served.

Abner Curry was a tough-hided rancher who had
muscled his way into the valley a couple of years before, and though Long Shadow suspected that Curry
had obtained his massive ranch through underhanded
means, the marshal had not been able to prove it. One
by one, other ranchers in the area had been selling
their spreads to Curry at rock-bottom prices and moving out, leading the lawman to believe that Curry wanted
to swallow up the entire valley and was making threats
to get the smaller ranchers to sell. . . . But so far not
one of the ranchers would admit the truth.

The brothers came through the Potters' gate, and
Long Shadow pulled rein and nodded coolly at them.
The Currys hauled up in turn, and their faces were

impassive as they exchanged terse greetings with the marshal. Bud Curry eyed the wounded prisoner, his slain cohort, and the dead deer and commented, "Looks like you've been doin' some fancy shootin'."

"Not me," Long Shadow replied, gesturing with his chin toward his boy. "Little Sun did all the shooting."

The Currys exchanged skeptical glances but none commented. "Well, we got chores to do at home," Bud finally said.

With that, the Curry brothers put spurs to their mounts and galloped away, heading eastward toward their ranch.

Bending low over his saddle horn, outlaw Walt Frick's interest seemed to perk up as the nine-year-old asked his father, "They sure are mean-looking men, aren't they?"

Leading the procession forward once again, Long Shadow replied, "That they are, son. That they are. And generally you can tell a lot about what is inside a man by the set of his face and the look in his eyes. A wise man once said that the eyes are the windows of the soul."

Little Sun reflected on his father's words for a few moments, then remarked, "Then Abner Curry must really have a bad soul. He's the meanest-looking Curry of all."

Although Long Shadow did not reply, he was thinking that a showdown was coming between himself and the Currys, as sure as darkness follows sunset.

Elvie Potter wept as the Curry brothers rode away. Watching her husband struggling to rise to his feet, she left the porch and shuffled toward him, saying, "Just a moment, dear. Let me help you."

Gripping the side of the trough and still coughing up

water, Clarence Potter responded, "No, honey. I'll make it. You go back and sit down." However, he was so weakened that he could not find the strength to pull himself up off his knees.

Elvie continued her slow shuffle. Reaching him, the old woman broke into sobs and wailed, "Those wicked brutes! They've hurt you, haven't they?" She took hold of one of Clarence's arms and attempted to help him rise.

"No, honey," the rancher insisted, shaking his head. "I'm just a little dizzy, that's all."

"Come, dear," Elvie persisted, tugging on his arm. "Let's get you in the house. Let's—" Suddenly a sensation that made her think of lightning sliced through her body. Falling to her knees next to her husband, she grabbed at her chest and collapsed.

"Elvie!" Clarence screamed. "Elvie!"

# Chapter Three

The sky was aglow with a brilliant sunset as Long Shadow led his group toward town. As they neared the outskirts of Cheyenne Crossing, the lawman sent his son on ahead to the doctors' office to inform them that he was bringing in a wounded prisoner.

Pulling his horse to an abrupt halt in front of the clinic, Little Sun slid from the saddle, quickly wrapped the reins around the hitch rail, and bolted up the walkway to the office door. Entering the dimly lit waiting room, he found no one but saw lamplight streaming beneath the door to the examining room.

In response to his knock, light, rapid footsteps sounded immediately. The door then opened to reveal Sally Easton Tottingham's pretty, fair face. Long Shadow's son had had a crush on the young physician since she and her doctor husband had opened their joint medical practice some six years earlier, and Sally—unaware of the boy's crush—sometimes inadvertently embarrassed him by calling him her boyfriend.

Smiling when she saw it was Little Sun at the door, the lovely blonde said, "Well, if it isn't my very special boyfriend!"

Little Sun's dark face deepened in color as he responded, "Hello, Aunt Sally."

Before Little Sun could say more, Sally reached out

and cupped his chin, examining the vertical stripes on his cheek. "Is that blood? Are you hurt?"

"It's blood," he answered levelly, "but I'm not hurt. I made my first kill as a hunter today, and it's my people's custom that when a boy makes his first kill, the blood of the animal is placed on his cheeks. My father put it there."

"Oh," she breathed with relief. "And what did you kill?"

"A big buck deer," he replied proudly. Looking past her, into the clinic, he asked, "Is Dr. Tottingham here"—he grinned—"the *other* Dr. Tottingham?"

"Not at the moment. Is something wrong?"

"My father is bringing in a prisoner who has a bullet in his shoulder. He sent me ahead to let you and Dr. Ron know. You once explained that you treat the ailments and Dr. Ron takes care of the surgeries. I guess removing a bullet is a surgery, right?"

"That's right. I am, of course, qualified to perform operations, but my husband is certainly the better surgeon of the two of us." She laughed, adding, "And he will definitely tell you that I have much the better bedside manner when it comes to ill patients."

"Will he be back soon?"

"He's at my father's store. Tell you what. Why don't you go get him? In the meantime, I'll prepare his surgical instruments."

"Yes, ma'am," the boy agreed and turned to leave.

Sally called after him, "Little Sun . . ."

Stopping, he turned about. "Yes, Aunt Sally?"

"Your father . . . did he have a shoot-out with this prisoner? I mean, your father is all right, isn't he?"

"He's fine, except for a split lip and a couple of bruises on his face." He briefly explained how the outlaws had gotten the jump on the lawman, then tied and beat him. The boy concluded, "But the other man was killed, and Papa says the prisoner will go to jail for a long, long time."

Sally's brow furrowed. "How did your father get loose and shoot them?"

Little Sun looked at the floor, then met her gaze as he answered, "He can tell you about it when he gets here. I'd better go get Dr. Ron." With that, he dashed out the door and hurried to the Cheyenne Crossing Mercantile Company two blocks away, which was owned by Sally's father, Ted Easton.

Knowing it would take her husband little more than five minutes to return, Sally quickly laid out his surgical instruments, antiseptic, ether, and the other items necessary for removing bullets from human bodies. As she did so, she thought of how much the boy resembled his father, and though Long Shadow had been five years older than Little Sun when she had first met him, there was a great deal about the boy that reminded her of the Indian youth she had fallen in love with when she was fourteen and years later almost married.

Memories flooded into her mind as she recalled those days when, believing his beloved April Dawn was dead, Long Shadow had finally courted her and they had then planned their wedding. The handsome Indian had been honest with her, telling her that he was still in love with April Dawn's cherished memory. But Sally had loved him so deeply that she wanted to marry him in spite of it, thinking that in time she could make him forget April Dawn and win his heart.

There was still a tinge of pain in Sally's breast as she thought of the day the beautiful Indian maiden came riding into Cheyenne Crossing, alive and well . . . just twenty-four hours before the wedding was to take place. It was like having her heart cut out to remove herself from Long Shadow's life and let him be with the woman with whom he really belonged.

A short time later Sally left Cheyenne Crossing to attend medical school in Kansas City, Missouri, an unusual decision for a woman. There she fell in love with Dr. Ronald L. Tottingham, who had come to the United States from England to teach medicine. Just after Sally finished school, word came from Cheyenne Crossing that the town's physician, Dr. Jacob Fryar, was retiring. Engaged by then, the couple discussed the opportunity, and Tottingham decided he would like to live and work on the frontier, so the couple took over Fryar's practice. Married in Kansas City just before leaving for Cheyenne Crossing, the Drs. Tottingham had now been working as a team in the town for six years.

Though Sally was very much in love with her tall, handsome husband, Long Shadow still held a special place in her heart. The good doctor knew and understood this, for her love and devotion to him were so full and complete that it was of no consequence, and in fact, Sally and April Dawn had become the closest of friends.

The brilliant hue of the sunset was fading as Long Shadow entered Cheyenne Crossing under the curious gaze of the townspeople, who gawked at the strange procession as it slowly passed by. A small crowd collected as the marshal hauled up in front of the clinic and dismounted.

"Hey, Marshal!" called out one man. "Looks like you've had a busy day!"

Ignoring him, Long Shadow motioned to a couple of men and said, "You fellas tie the horses, will you? I've got to get this man inside fast."

The men quickly obliged as Long Shadow helped Walt Frick from his saddle. Frick was so weak he could not stand, and the lawman threw the outlaw's good arm over his shoulder and half carried him. As he was about to open the door, he saw Ronald Tottingham coming up the street at a fast walk with Little Sun beside him, his short legs laboring to keep up with the tall physician's long strides.

The door abruptly opened and Sally stood there. "I have everything ready," she said softly, surveying the prisoner's pain-contorted face. "Ron should be here any moment. I sent Little Sun to fetch him."

"As a matter of fact, he's almost here," Long Shadow responded.

Ushering the marshal and his prisoner into the clinic, Sally directed Long Shadow to lay Frick on the operating table. While he was doing so, she eyed the Indian and remarked, "That split lip is swollen, Long Shadow, and those bruises could use some looking at, too."

Nodding at Frick, the Indian replied, "Let's get him taken care of first."

Removing Frick's hat, Sally tossed it onto a chair and immediately began cutting away his bloody shirt with a pair of scissors. Frick gritted his teeth and grunted, "I'm really hurtin', lady. You got some whiskey?"

"The doctor will be here in a few seconds," Sally replied coldly, knowing what the man had done to Long Shadow. "He'll take care of your pain." As she spoke, Tottingham's footsteps sounded in the waiting room, along with those of Little Sun, and presently they came through the door.

The boy hurried to his father as the doctor greeted Long Shadow and went immediately to Frick. Dr. Tottingham took a quick look at the bullet wound, then washed his hands, telling Sally over his shoulder to administer the ether. Frick insisted on whiskey rather than anesthetic, but as Sally removed the lid from the bottle and poured the liquid into a large cloth—filling

the room with ether fumes—she said quietly, "No whiskey, mister. Just be glad for ether. You won't feel a
thing while the doctor digs that bullet out." Sally laid
the cloth over the outlaw's face, and there was no more
argument from Frick.

Drying his hands on a sterilized towel, Tottingham
said, "Marshal, your boy told me that he had to kill one
outlaw and shoot your prisoner here in order to keep
them from killing you. That must have been quite an
ordeal for both of you."

Sally's face paled. Looking up from her patient, she
stared first at Little Sun, then at Long Shadow, and
back again at the boy. "You had to kill a man?" she
asked quietly.

The boy nodded wordlessly.

"He had no choice," the lawman interjected. Laying
a hand on the boy's shoulder, he replied, "I sent Frick
to prison seven years ago, and he recently got out and
came to get even by killing me. He and his partner took
me unawares in the forest, but fortunately Little Sun
came to my rescue and saved my life. I am very proud
of him for his courage."

The Tottinghams got down to work, with Sally treat-
ing Long Shadow's facial bruises with iodine and salve
while her husband cleaned the area around Frick's wound
in preparation for removing the bullet. Joining him,
Sally assisted as Tottingham started to probe for the
slug.

Long Shadow watched the procedure, then asked,
"When will I be able to jail my prisoner, Ron?"

"I should think I can release him to you in a couple of
days."

"Where will you keep him?"

Pointing to a small room just off the examining and
operating room, the doctor replied, "In there."

Long Shadow stepped to the door of the room and looked in, noting the room contained a metal bed with side rails. Nodding, he said, "That'll be excellent." He pulled a pair of handcuffs from his hip pocket, adding, "When you're finished, I can shackle him to the side rail."

Tottingham merely nodded and kept working. Finally the operation was completed, and the lawman assisted the physician in carrying Frick into the back room. Long Shadow had just finished handcuffing the outlaw to the bed when footsteps sounded in the waiting room. A moment later Clarence Potter shuffled into the examining room, worry etched on his weathered face.

Nodding briefly and nervously at the marshal, the old man called to Tottingham, "Elvie's out in the wagon, and she's real bad. Is it okay if I bring her in?"

In the middle of washing the blood from his instruments, Tottingham paused and looked over at his wife, who acknowledged his glance with a rueful little smile. Like many of the people in and around Cheyenne Crossing, especially the older ones, Clarence Potter could not accept the fact that Sally Tottingham was as qualified a physician as her husband. The doctors had resigned themselves to the fact that certain of their patients would always prefer—if not insist—that their ailments and broken bones be treated by the *male* Dr. Tottingham.

Knowing how Clarence felt, Sally immediately suggested that she attend to the cleaning of the surgical instruments so that her husband could attend Elvie Potter.

Tottingham dried his hands and walked over to the rancher, asking, "What is it, Clarence? Is Elvie sick?"

Clarence's lower lip began quivering. "She's sick, all right, Doc. Real sick. I think it's her heart."

Nodding his head toward the examining table across the room, Tottingham said, "Bring her in and put her over there."

The rancher was pale and shaky on his feet, and Long Shadow suggested, "Grab a chair and sit down, Clarence. I'll bring Elvie in."

While Clarence sat, rubbing his temples with a trembling hand, Long Shadow carried a half-conscious Elvie Potter into the clinic and laid her on the examining table. The lamplight revealed that her face was ashen gray, and her breath was coming in short spurts while her right hand clutched her dress just over her heart. Sally took over the cleaning, and Tottingham hurried to the old woman's side, checking her pulse and listening with his stethoscope to her heart.

Something in Clarence's demeanor compelled Long Shadow to stay until the doctor made his diagnosis. April Dawn would just have to wait a little longer to know that her husband and son were all right. The old man held tight to his chair while Tottingham listened to Elvie's heart and checked other vital signs. After several minutes, the physician declared, "She's definitely had a heart seizure, Clarence. When did it happen?"

"Uh . . . about four-thirty or so," responded the old-ster, wiping sweat from his brow. "Maybe . . . maybe even five or a bit after. I . . . I'm not sure. Sometime late this afternoon. It happened while she was outside, and I helped her into the house and made her lie down. After a while, I realized it was bad, so I brought her here as fast as I could."

"Was there anything in particular that brought it on?" Tottingham asked. "A sudden shock or something that frightened her?"

Watching the old man intently, it was obvious to Long Shadow that Clarence was terrified. But the rancher

merely stammered, "Nothing that . . . that I can think
of, Doc."

The marshal recalled the look of triumph on the faces
of the Curry brothers as they were coming out of the
Potters' gate, and he stepped to the rancher and looked
down at him. "What were Bud, Jake, and Reese Curry
doing at your place today, Clarence?" he demanded.

The oldster's head jerked up. His lower lip quivered
as he said, "Oh. Well, they . . . uh . . . just came by
for a neighborly visit."

"It was well after five o'clock when I saw them at
your gate. Did Elvie have the problem when they were
there?"

Clarence evaded Long Shadow's piercing gaze. Rubbing the back of his neck, he insisted, "No. No, it
wasn't till some time after they were gone that the pain
hit her. I . . . I guess it was later than I thought."

Long Shadow did not believe the old man. He was
certain the Currys had been there to frighten him into
selling out, and the look in Clarence's eyes bore out his
suspicion. Asking that he be kept informed of Elvie's
condition, Long Shadow left with Little Sun on his
heels to take Harry Denker's body to the undertaker
and then go home.

While six-year-old Star Light was waiting at the front
of the house, peering through the window for some sign
of her father and brother, April Dawn was in the kitchen,
laboring to keep supper from burning and her worry
from turning to fear. Looking down the hall at her
daughter, the beautiful Cheyenne smiled. Star Light
was a duplicate of her mother, having the same long
black hair, flashing black eyes, and small, delicate frame.

As the child stood glued to the window, it was clear
that her mother's worry for the safety of Long Shadow

and Little Sun picked at Star Light's mind as well.
Suddenly above the soft night sounds of crickets and
the wind came the clopping of hooves. Star Light ran to
the door, pulled it open, and hurried onto the front
porch.

"Papa?" called the child. "Is that you?"

"Yes, it is!" Long Shadow called.

Hearing her husband's voice, April Dawn felt the
knot of worry in her chest instantly dissolve. She wiped
her hands on her apron and strode to the front door just
as Star Light shouted happily, "Mama! Papa and Little
Sun are back!"

Long Shadow and Little Sun were dismounting when
mother and daughter hurried toward them. While Star
Light rushed into her father's arms, April Dawn embraced her son, her gaze falling on the dead buck. "I
see you were successful in your hunt," she said in a
voice filled with pride. "Is that what made you so late?"

Long Shadow kissed his wife and asked, "May we
explain it to you over supper?"

Relieved to have them home safely, the lovely woman
nodded and said, "Of course. It may be somewhat
burnt and dried out, but I guess we can still eat it."

When they entered the well-lit house, April Dawn
immediately saw that Long Shadow's face had been
beaten, and she pressed him to tell her what had happened. "I'm sure you're as hungry as we are," he responded. "Let's start eating, and I'll explain it all then."

At the table, Long Shadow told the whole story. First
boasting about his son's excellent hunting skills, he
then told them about the incident with the two outlaws.
April Dawn was grieved to learn that Little Sun had
been forced to kill a man but was deeply grateful that
her boy had the courage to save his father's life. She
was also disturbed to hear of Elvie Potter's heart seizure.

After a subdued dinner, the tightly knit family gathered in the barn. They preferred doing things together whenever possible, and everyone watched while Long Shadow dressed out the deer.

Little Sun stood very close to his father, his eyes huge. Declaring that he planned to become a great hunter and that therefore this was something he had to know, he observed carefully. Star Light, on the other hand, hovered close to her mother, clearly finding the bloody sight repugnant. Oblivious to the gore, April Dawn sat on a nail keg a few feet away, her eyes fixed on the man she loved. The yellow light from the lanterns glossed his handsome face, painting him with flickering shadows.

Watching her husband, she mulled over his comments about the Curry brothers and the Potters. Long Shadow was dropping entrails into a galvanized tub, and April Dawn was about to ask what he was going to do about the Currys, when a British-accented male voice called out, "Hello! My word, that's as bloody as *our* work!"

April Dawn looked over to see Ronald Tottingham standing in the open doorway. She immediately stood and walked across the barn to greet him, but her smile faded as she read the expression on the physician's handsome face.

"What is it, Ron?" she asked.

"Bad news, I'm afraid. Elvie Potter died a few minutes ago."

April Dawn groaned and said, "Poor Mr. Potter. He's going to be so lonely."

"That he will. Sally's with him right now at the clinic, but he'll have to leave soon and go back to his empty house."

Continuing with his task, Long Shadow remarked, "I

can't prove it, but I'd bet anything that Elvie's heart seizure was brought on by the Currys' visit today. We've discussed this before, Ron, and we both know what Abner and his sons are doing. Clarence is terrified. I'm sure you noticed that."

Tottingham closed his eyes and nodded. "I'm certain that something traumatic brought on Elvie's seizure . . . and I'm as sure as you that it was a threat by the Currys. I just wish you could get Clarence to admit it."

His work on the deer finished, Long Shadow laid down the knife and began washing the blood from his hands in a bucket of water. Looking over his shoulder at his wife, he told her, "I am going to the clinic to talk to Clarence again. If I can get him to tell me the truth, it'll give me grounds to arrest the Currys for extortion— and perhaps I even have grounds for an involuntary manslaughter charge."

Clarence Potter was seated beside the table where his wife's body lay when the marshal entered the clinic. Long Shadow crossed the room and rested a hand on the old man's shoulder, expressing his sympathy. Clarence wept for a few minutes, then dried his tears with a large bandanna.

Pulling up a chair, the lawman sat down and looked the old man in the eye. "Please be honest with me, Clarence," he insisted. "The Currys were there to frighten you and Elvie into selling your ranch to them at a ridiculous price, were they not?"

The rancher looked at the floor but did not reply.

The marshal pressed him. "Did they threaten you? Tell you not to say anything to me or they'd hurt you? Is that what frightened Elvie so?"

Shaking his head, Clarence mumbled, "No, Marshal. You've got it all wrong. They only came by to pay a friendly visit."

Touching the old man's arm, Long Shadow said, "Listen, you don't have to be afraid. I won't let them hurt you. If you'll just tell me the truth, I can put them behind bars."

But the rancher's fear, which was written all over him, would not allow him to incriminate them.

Quietly leaving the clinic, barely keeping his fury in check, the marshal headed home. He would saddle up and ride to the Curry ranch, for even though he could not arrest them without Clarence Potter's testimony, perhaps his presence alone would throw a scare into them.

Rose Johnson, the middle-aged woman whom the widowed Abner Curry had hired as a housekeeper, had supper cooking and was setting the table when the youngest son, Emmett, strolled into the kitchen. In dire need of the job—which the Currys knew—the plump, fair-haired woman never let her true feelings toward the ranchers show, nor did she ever criticize them. Smiling at the tall, slender Emmett, she told him, "I've fixed your favorite this evening—chicken and dumplings."

"Sounds good," the twenty-year-old responded.

Bud, Jake, and Reese suddenly piled into the kitchen, smelling of horse and saddle leather. Jake asked Rose what they were having for supper, and when she told him, he commented to Emmett that the housekeeper spoiled him as much as their father did.

Ignoring the remark, Emmett asked, "How'd it go at the Potters'?"

Jake was about to reply when Abner Curry, whistling a nameless tune, could be heard coming toward the kitchen from his den near the front of the house.

Short and very stocky, with the same sloping bull-like shoulders and thick neck he had passed on to his middle sons, the senior Curry entered the kitchen. Abner looked his boys over, then looked up at his oldest son and asked, "You get Potter to agree to sell?"

"Not quite, Pa," Bud replied, his face flushing slightly. "But he's thinkin' it over right now."

Glancing at Rose, Abner lowered his voice. "Have to rough him up?"

"A little."

"A *little*?" Jake snorted. "He practically drowned the old geezer in the water trough!"

Reese chuckled. "Shook the old lady up, too!"

Her own face darkening—though from anger at their cruelty rather than embarrassment—Rose spoke up, "If you *gentlemen* will clear a path, I will put the food on the table."

Moments later, the five men sat at the table and began wolfing down the food. Not bothering to swallow before speaking, Abner asked, "So how soon you goin' back to talk to Potter again, Bud?"

"I told him we'd be back in a couple of days. But maybe we oughta wait a bit longer."

"Why?" the rancher demanded.

" 'Cause Long Shadow saw us there."

The patriarch's eyes widened. "Long Shadow saw you on Potter's property?"

"Yeah. Just as we were leavin', there he was, passin' by the place. Had his kid with him, and a couple of outlaws. Least I assumed they were outlaws. He never really said. One was dead, and the other was shot up bad."

"He ask you what you were doin' at the Potters'?"

"Nope. Nary a word. We just passed the time of day real quick and kept on movin'." He paused, then added

ominously, "But there was a look in that stinkin' Indian's eye. I know he suspects what we're doin', Pa."

"So what?" Abner blared. "As long as we keep people
scared spitless, he ain't gonna find nothin' out—and I
think he's tried every way possible to prove it."

"You're right about that," Bud said with a grin. "So
far he ain't been able to touch us, even though we've
scared five families into sellin' to us real cheap. Fear is
a wonderful thing, you know that?"

There was a round of coarse laughter; then Jake
added, "And as long as we can keep people afraid of us,
nobody'll stop us from takin' over this whole valley."

"That's what I want for my boys," Abner said. "I've
told you before: I want to see each of you boys ownin' a
spread of at least a hundred thousand acres."

After supper, the Currys sat on the front porch of the
huge ranch house, smoking cigarettes and sipping brandy.
The moon was rising, and they could hear the ranch
hands laughing and talking in the bunkhouse across the
yard.

No one spoke for a while. Then Abner remarked,
"Bud, I don't want you wastin' time with old man
Potter. Next time you go there, I want results, even if
you have to rough the old lady up a bit. You break that
old duffer and you break him quick, hear me?"

"Don't worry about it, Pa," Bud replied, flicking
ashes from his cigarette. "Old Clarence looked like a
drowned rat when I got through with him. He'll crack
the minute he sees us comin'. I guarantee you, he's
thinkin' about our little visit right now. He ain't about
to jeopardize the old lady's welfare."

Abner laughed fiendishly. "Good! That means the
Potter place will soon be mine!"

Waiting till his father's laughter subsided, Reese suggested, "I think we oughta go after Brown's place next, Pa. He just built a big new barn, and—"

At the sound of hoofbeats, Reese stopped speaking. A ghostly-looking horse and rider materialized on the moon-lit prairie, and the Currys squinted, trying to make out who it was.

Flicking his cigarette into the dust, Abner asked, "Any of our boys go to town this afternoon?"

"No, Pa," Emmett replied. "Everybody's been on the place since just past noon. Guess we got us a visitor."

Peering at the approaching rider, Reese recognized the white hat and fringed buckskin shirt. Swearing, he growled, "It's Long Shadow!"

Abner shook his head. "What it is," he growled, "is trouble. I can smell it."

# Chapter Four

Abner Curry and his four sons rose to their feet as Marshal Long Shadow reined in and swung from his saddle. Before the Cheyenne could speak, Abner demanded, "What do you want, Marshal?"

Ignoring the question, Long Shadow stepped onto the porch, planting himself in front of the three brothers he had seen earlier in the day. Glaring at Bud, Jake, and Reese, he demanded, "What were you doing at the Potter place this afternoon?"

Reese, the toughest and flintiest of the bunch, bristled. "That's none of your business, lawman!"

Long Shadow stiffened. "You're wrong, mister!" he countered hotly. "It *is* my business!"

The pale moonlight seemed to accentuate the hostility evident on Reese's beefy face, and the look in his eyes was wild and ruthless. "Is it against the law for neighbors to make friendly visits to each other?"

"It is when the visit carries threats of bodily harm," the marshal replied, "and causes an old woman to have a heart seizure and die!"

The Currys immediately fell quiet, glancing at each other. Finally the rancher broke the uncomfortable silence by asking, "Are you tellin' us that Elvie Potter died after my sons were there?"

"That's exactly what I'm telling you!" Long Shadow

exclaimed. "In the language of the law, that comes under the heading of involuntary manslaughter."

"Now, look here, Marshal!" Reese shouted. "You ain't—"

"Hold it, Reese," his father cautioned, touching his arm. Facing the marshal, Abner stated flatly, "This manslaughter charge would only hold if my sons were guilty of makin' threats, ain't that right? Did Clarence Potter say the visit was unfriendly and my boys threatened him and Elvie?"

There was a brief pause, and then Long Shadow admitted, "He didn't come right out and say anything like that, but I could read the fear in his eyes."

"Bah!" Abner exclaimed. "You're graspin' at straws. I resent you comin' on my property and insinuatin' that my boys would threaten an old man and woman and cause her death!"

"Yeah!" Reese blared, his face beet red. "Don't try to pin this manslaughter stuff on us. We didn't have nothin' to do with it!"

Stepping close to Reese and towering over him, Long Shadow muttered through clenched teeth, "I know that you *did*, mister—just as I know the bunch of you have frightened other small ranchers in this valley so they'd sell their spreads to you cheap. I can't prove it—not yet. But I will."

Abner Curry swore. Pushing himself between Reese and Long Shadow, he bellowed heatedly, "Why, you snake-bellied Indian! You got no business wearin' a white man's badge! You belong on the reservation in Montana with the rest of the Cheyenne vermin!"

Fire leapt into Long Shadow's eyes, but he struggled to suppress his fury.

Spraying saliva as he railed fiercely, Abner continued, "You can't arrest me for hatin' your Indian guts, lawman, and you can't arrest Bud, Jake, and Reese for payin' a friendly call on our neighbors! So why don't you just get on your horse and ride? The Indian smell is startin' to get to me."

Still fighting to contain his anger, Long Shadow growled, "I'm warning you, Curry. Don't you or your boys threaten any more ranchers. Sooner or later I'm going to get proof of the extortion you've already committed, and when I do, I'm going to nail your hides to the door . . . all of you!"

With those words hanging in the night air, Long Shadow pivoted and stepped off the porch. Suddenly Reese jumped in front of him, insolence written all over his face.

Long Shadow halted. "Get out of my way."

Dropping his cigarette butt and grinding it beneath his boot heel, Reese stared coldly up at the tall lawman. "Why don't you take off that badge, *Indian dog*? Let's you and me have it out man to man."

Long Shadow scowled at Reese, then rasped, "I said, get out of my way!"

But the burly man did not move. Squaring his box-like shoulders, Reese sneered, "Whatsa matter, redskin? Or do I have it wrong? Maybe your skin is yellow . . . especially your belly. You willin' to fight me bare-knuckled, man to man?" Smirking, he added tauntingly, "If you're half a man, not just stinkin' Indian vermin, you'll take off that badge and fight me."

Though wanting to punch out the man in the worst way, Long Shadow knew that to do so on Curry property could cause serious complications, for undoubtedly the clan would insist that the marshal had abused the rights conferred by his position, and charges would be leveled against him. He could lose his badge.

His cheeks pulsing as he clenched his teeth, the

lawman stepped around Reese and strode to his horse. Mounting, he rode away.

Reese's coarse laughter rode the night air as he shouted mockingly, "Just as I thought! You're a yellow, snake-bellied Indian coward!" Chuckling triumphantly, he climbed onto the porch and sat back in his chair to a chorus of approval from his brothers. "I guess I sent him packin'. I'd say we've seen the last of that coward."

But his father shook his head slowly, then remarked, "You're wrong about that, boy."

The laughter died instantly. The Curry brothers eyed each other questioningly, then looked at the patriarch, waiting for him to explain.

"What do you mean, Pa?" Reese asked.

The rancher grumbled, "That Indian wasn't afraid of you. If he'd taken you up on your challenge, you'd be lyin' there in the dirt, probably minus some teeth and a half-pint of blood."

Reese Curry looked at his father as though he was seeing him for the first time in his life. "That skinny bean pole whip *me*? Shoot, I got forty pounds on him! You are joshin' me, ain't you, Pa?"

"No, I ain't. He's a lawman through and through. No sensible lawman's gonna come onto private property and be goaded into a fistfight. He knows all too well it wouldn't look good for him if we decided to press charges."

"Okay, then," Reese rejoined, grinning, "I'll just take him on somewhere on neutral ground."

Frowning, Abner declared, "You don't listen too good, do you, boy? I'm tellin' you, that Indian ain't nobody you want to fight. I've seen him at it a couple of times in town. You keep your distance from him. He's got fists like sledgehammers."

"Look, Pa," Reese insisted, "we gotta do somethin' about that red scum. He's gonna mess up our plans. You heard him. He's on to us. It's only a matter of time till he nails us. I think I'll just kill him."

Abner's face grew hard and his eyes narrowed. "Don't you try it! That redskin has eyes in the back of his head. Do you know how many men have tried to kill him, just in the two years we've been here? Every one of 'em's lyin' dead in the ground. It's like his heathen gods are protectin' him all the time, or somethin'. Don't none of you boys *ever* try killin' him!" he said fiercely, running his gaze over the faces of his sons. "You boys have been my whole life since your ma died. I couldn't stand it if one of you was killed."

Reese leaned over and patted the rancher's shoulder, saying, "I won't try to kill him, Pa, but I sure would like a chance to rearrange his Cheyenne features for him."

Shaking his head, Abner warned, "Forget it, son. I'm tellin' you, he's tougher'n you think. We'll just have to be real careful from now on, that's all." Rising to his feet, he added, "Well, it's bedtime for your old man. See you boys at the breakfast table."

The Curry brothers remained on the porch. When their father was well into the house and out of earshot, Reese said to the others, "I ain't interested in meetin' Long Shadow gun for gun, but I'd like to take him on fist for fist. I don't care what Pa says. I can whip that stinkin' savage."

"Sure you can," Bud agreed. "Pa ain't seen you in a fight in a long time. He just don't know how fast you are with your fists and how hard you can punch."

"Be more fun takin' the lawman on in town, anyway," Reese mused, grinning. "That way I can embarrass him in front of all them folks who think he's so great."

Looking doubtful, Jake interjected, "What if, because of that badge, he still won't fight you? It probably wouldn't shame him at all if he backed off from a fight, even there in town, 'cause he's a lawman."

Scratching at the back of his thick neck, Reese mumbled, "Then I gotta figure a way to force him into a fight, 'cause I ain't gonna rest till I've pounded that snake-bellied scum into the dirt."

Emmett chuckled. "I can tell you a surefire way to get him to fight you, big brother. You ever notice how devoted he is to that gorgeous wife of his? Well, you insult her a little and you'll have your fight."

A wide, evil grin spread over Reese Curry's face. "Yeah," he said maliciously. "That'd do it!"

It was midmorning the next day, and Reese Curry and two of the hired hands were sharing a bottle of whiskey in the Rusty Lantern Saloon when Emmett Curry rushed in.

"Hey, big brother," he announced, his eyes gleaming, "I just saw Long Shadow's wife goin' into the mercantile store. Now's your chance."

Throwing back the rest of the amber liquid in his glass, Reese stood, wiped his mouth, and grinned. "It sure is," he responded and hurried through the batwing doors. His youngest brother and the cowhands were hot on his heels, smiling in expectation.

Walking at a brisk pace, Reese led them down the street and stopped in front of Ted Easton's store. Telling the others to move away from him, he stood at the edge of the boardwalk and waited for April Dawn to appear. Some fifteen minutes had passed when Reese, increasingly impatient, called to Emmett. "Do me a favor and go see if that squaw is still inside."

Emmett had just started toward the door when it

opened and April Dawn emerged, carrying several small packages. The door was held ajar by her son, while her daughter carried her mother's purse.

Emmett immediately stepped out of the way, grinning knowingly at the ranch hands. The burly Reese went into action, strolling casually toward April Dawn but looking in the opposite direction, acting as if he did not see her. Suddenly he collided with her, and her packages flew from her grasp and fell to the boardwalk.

Staggering slightly, the Indian woman quickly regained her balance and glared at Reese, who stood with his hands on his hips, looking her up and down. Grinning salaciously, he said in a mocking tone, "Well, pardon me."

April Dawn's eyes sparked as she snapped, "You did that on purpose! I will thank you to pick up my packages!"

Chuckling insolently, Reese kicked the packages out of the way and grabbed April Dawn by the shoulders. Before she could react, he planted his mouth on hers, kissing fiercely while she struggled to free herself.

Star Light began to cry, while Little Sun, his fury ignited, began to kick Reese in the legs, shouting, "Let go of my mother! Let go of my mother!"

One of the bystanders quickly raced to the marshal's office, summoning the lawman. Long Shadow, his face dark with rage, flew out of his office and raced along the boardwalk. He neared the mercantile store in time to see Reese, annoyed by Little Sun's assault, release April Dawn and slap the boy hard across the face, hissing, "I'll teach you, Indian brat!" The boy was sent tumbling into the street by the impact of the blow, and a red mark rose on his cheek.

Black eyes blazing, Long Shadow stormed up to Reese and snarled, "You disgusting slime! You put your filthy mouth on my wife and you hit my son! Nobody touches my family, Curry! Nobody!"

A large crowd was rapidly forming, and among the onlookers were Frank Denton, the bank president and town council chairman, and gunsmith Barry Hawkins, who wore the deputy's badge. They eyed each other warily as Reese, his jaw jutting, squared himself with the marshal and retorted contemptuously, "Nobody, eh? Well, I just did, lawman. There ain't no law on the books that says I can't kiss a squaw or smack a redskin brat, is there, Marshal? I mean, you can't arrest me for those kinds of pleasures, can you?"

Long Shadow's muscular chest was heaving with suppressed rage. Gritting his teeth, he breathed hotly, "So you really want a fight that bad, eh?"

Narrowing his eyes, the thick-bodied man laughed maliciously and replied, "Yeah, I sure do."

"Well, you are getting your wish," Long Shadow responded, taking off his badge. Turning to Frank Denton, he handed him the shiny six-pointed star and said, "I'm taking a brief leave of absence. Barry is officially marshal until I put this badge back on. What I'm about to do will be as a private citizen—husband of my wife and father of my son."

Eyes shining eagerly, Reese stepped to the center of the street and shouted, "Come on, Indian yellow-belly. Let's get on with it!"

Long Shadow stepped momentarily to April Dawn and said, "I'm going to fix him so he won't be able to kiss anybody for a long time."

Clutching her still-frightened daughter, April Dawn nodded silently. Long Shadow stroked Star Light's soft face and said soothingly, "It's all right, now, honey. That mean man won't hurt you or your mama." Leaning over and placing his palm against Little Sun's reddened cheek, he breathed, "I'm proud of you for trying to help your mother—and I'll teach Reese Curry a lesson for both of us."

The Cheyenne boy grinned and said, "Teach him good, Papa."

The crowd waited with obvious anticipation as their marshal moved toward the big man in the center of the street. Reese rolled his massive shoulders, then took off his hat, tossed it to his brother, and winked. Emmett smiled and winked back. As Reese squared himself with Long Shadow, he saw Ronald Tottingham in the crowd and called, "Hey, Doc! Better stay close! This yellow-bellied redskin is gonna need you real soon!"

Standing six feet away, Long Shadow growled, "Perhaps you should shut your mouth and start fighting."

Smirking, Reese came at Long Shadow with a wild roar, his fists pumping. The lithe marshal dodged two punches meant to devastate him and lashed out with a blow that caught Reese flush on the mouth. The young rancher's head snapped back, and there was utter surprise in his eyes. Before he could recover, Long Shadow slugged him viciously on the jaw, whipping his head sideways, then slugged him again on the rebound.

Reese went down, flat on his back, while Long Shadow stood waiting for him to rise. Rolling onto his knees, Reese shook his head repeatedly, and when he finally stood, there was murder in his eyes. His upper lip was split and bleeding, and when he ran a sleeve over his mouth and saw the blood, his rage intensified. Roaring again, he bolted forward, throwing the full weight of his bulk into Long Shadow's body. They connected, and the Indian went down with Reese on top of him. The heavier man attempted to get a stranglehold, but Long Shadow was too fast, and he countered by slamming the big man in the nose with an elbow, stunning him.

Long Shadow took advantage of the moment and flipped the bulky man off him. Reese suddenly grabbed the Indian's ankle and twisted it, but Long Shadow used his other foot to kick his opponent square on the mouth. Reese fell backward, letting out a moan.

Rising, Long Shadow stood over the big man and rasped, "Get up, Reese! You aren't finished paying for what you did to my wife and son!"

When Reese finally stood, both lips were split and blood dripped from his chin onto his shirt. Vowing, "I'm gonna smash you, vermin!" he rushed at Long Shadow, swinging a powerful right. But the lawman met him with a powerful slam of his own, getting the upper hand.

The contest went on for several more minutes. At one point Deputy Hawkins wanted to stop the fight by clouting Reese on the head, but Frank Denton convinced him that Long Shadow would want to see it through to the bitter end—no matter what the outcome.

April Dawn, still holding her daughter, watched fearfully, but her eyes expressed her confidence that her husband would best his opponent. Emmett Curry was equally confident, and he waved his hands ecstatically, shouting, "Crush that Indian scum, Reese! Crush him!"

The mocking words gave Long Shadow the extra impetus he needed. As he visualized again the thick-bodied rancher's mouth on April Dawn's and his massive palm striking Little Sun's face, a fresh desire for vengeance rushed through the lawman. He hauled back and let loose with a punch that sent shock waves up his arm—and sent Reese Curry reeling.

"That was for hitting my son!" Long Shadow roared. Then, grabbing Reese's shirt, he hauled him to his feet, declaring, "And this is for kissing my wife!" The punch threw Reese onto his back.

To the cheers of the crowd, the vengeful Cheyenne leapt on top of his foe. Sinking his fingers into Reese's hair, he hissed, "You like to kiss, Reese? Well, kiss the ground!" With that, he turned the big man over and rammed his face full force into the hard dirt of the street. The young rancher tried to free himself from Long Shadow's grip, but he did not have the strength.

Long Shadow repeatedly pounded Reese's face into the dirt until he was out cold. Breathing hard, the marshal finally flipped his opponent onto his back. The younger man's face was a bloody mass. "Guess you won't be kissing anybody for quite a while," the Indian muttered to his unconscious foe.

The crowd was cheering as the lawman got to his feet and strode to his family, putting his arm protectively around his wife. With the help of his ranch hands, a stunned Emmett picked up his brother and started to carry him to the doctors' clinic when Reese began moaning and flailing his head, coming to. "Wait a minute, Emmett!" Long Shadow shouted. "Bring him over here."

Grudgingly obeying, the three men carried Reese over to where Long Shadow stood with his family. The marshal looked down at his opponent, who looked back with glazed eyes, and demanded, "You owe my wife and son an apology, mister. Let's hear it!"

His lips bleeding and puffy, Reese Curry mumbled an apology. As the rancher was carried away toward the clinic, Long Shadow called after him, "Nobody touches my family! Nobody!"

# Chapter Five

Two days later, when Marshal Long Shadow entered the jail cellblock, he found Walt Frick lying on his bunk, reading an old newspaper. The lawman stepped to the bars, and the outlaw eyed him balefully.

"Good news, Frick."

Sitting up, his arm in a sling, Frick spit a stream of tobacco juice into a coffee can on the floor and glumly asked, "What good news could you possibly have for me? I'm stuck in this stinkin' place, ain't I?"

"True. But I'm sure the food's better here than it is in prison, and it isn't as gloomy as the penitentiary, right?"

"Yeah, I'll give you that."

"Well, that's my good news. I can't send you back to prison till you have your trial, and I just received word that the circuit judge has taken sick. This region is shorthanded when it comes to judges, which means you're going to have to sit it out here until the regular judge recovers and can make it to Cheyenne Crossing."

"Whoopee," Frick responded sarcastically, lying back down. "Somehow the choice between your jail and the state prison don't seem like much of one."

Shrugging, the tall Indian commented, "You're right, it isn't. The real choice was the one you made several years ago, when you could have opted to do honest work instead of stealing from others."

Turning his back to Long Shadow, Frick said tartly, "You're a lawman, not a preacher—so don't preach to me."

The lawman shrugged again, then wheeled and left Frick to his solitude.

Abner Curry stood on the front porch of his huge ranch house with young Emmett standing beside him, watching his other three sons mount up and settle in their saddles. Reese's battered face was a gruesome-looking patchwork of stitches and various-colored bruises that ranged from yellow to purple.

Speaking with difficulty through his swollen lips, Reese remarked, "Pa, I think we ought to go after Darrell Brown's ranch next. You ain't seen his new barn yet. It's somethin' to behold."

"I told you the Furman place is next, Reese," Abner stated.

"But, Pa—"

"Hey!" the patriarch snapped, his tone suddenly harsh. "When are you gonna learn to listen to me, boy? If you'd heeded my warnin' about tryin' to take that Indian on, you wouldn't be lookin' like he worked your face over with a dull tomahawk. Your old man's still got some good sense left. The Furman place is more important than the Brown ranch 'cause it borders the Potter place—and when we get 'em both linked together, it'll give us one decent-sized spread. Got it?"

"Oh," Reese mumbled submissively. "I get it now."

Abner sighed. "Good. Now, you boys go convince Furman that his mother's callin' him back home to Illinois."

Bud, Jake, and Reese put their horses to a gallop and were in sight of the Furman place within fifteen minutes. Easing the animals to a walk, they rode up to the house, where Mel Furman, who would turn forty his next birthday, was working on his wagon, packing the wheels with fresh grease. Hearing the trio ride in, he looked up; seeing who his visitors were, he glared at them.

Nancy Furman and her two daughters, twelve and fourteen in age, were washing clothes and hanging them on a line beside the house. When the Curry brothers came into the yard, they stopped what they were doing and watched with trepidation.

A cow bawled in the corral as the three men drew rein. Before they could leave their saddles, Furman told them tightly, "No need to dismount. We have nothing to talk about. Go bother someone else."

Ignoring the rancher's directive, Bud Curry swung his leg over his saddle and slid to the ground. His brothers followed suit as Bud stepped close to Furman and, with a mock expression of hurt on his face, said, "Mel, is that any way to treat your neighbors? We come by to make a friendly call, and you bite our heads off."

As Nancy instructed her daughters to stay where they were, then headed toward her husband, Furman put down the can of grease that was in his hands and picked up a rag. Wiping his fingers, he said coldly, "Don't give me that 'friendly call' stuff, Curry. I know what you're here for, and the ranch isn't for sale . . . at *any* price." Turning his back to the threesome, he growled, "Don't let the gate hit your horse's rump on the way out."

Reese stepped in front of Furman, scowling. "We're here to make you a real good offer. There ain't no need for you to get nasty. At least listen to what we have to say."

Before the rancher could respond, Bud spoke up.

"We figure you've got somewheres around three hundred acres here, right?"

"Three hundred and forty," Furman corrected coolly, "and there's not even a dirt clod for sale."

"We're prepared to give you five thousand," Bud stated, ignoring the remark.

Looking at his wife, the rancher shook his head. "See, honey? I told you that when they came around to us, they'd make an offer so ridiculous it would be laughable."

Reese's temper flared. Reaching out, he gripped Furman's shirt at the shoulder, but the rancher batted his hand away and ordered the brothers off his property. Undaunted, Reese looked over at the two girls and asked menacingly, "You have three kids, don't you, Furman?"

Furman stiffened, and fear leapt into Nancy's face. Eyeing Reese levelly, he replied, "Yeah. So what?"

"Where's your boy?"

"None of your business. What are you driving at?"

"I bet you'd like to see that boy and those pretty girls grow up and give you some grandchildren for your old age, wouldn't you?"

The rancher's eyes narrowed. He held Reese's gaze but did not answer.

Reese continued, "You'd better reconsider our offer. If you don't make the right decision— Well, I think you get my drift."

Nancy Furman's eyes filled with tears and her face pinched with fear. Her voice shaky, she declared, "You wouldn't harm our children!"

"Of course not, ma'am. But accidents do happen."

Mel Furman's eyes sparked angrily and he exploded, "You touch our children and you'll answer to the law!"

Bud's stare was piercing as he told the Furmans

threateningly, "Goin' to the law for help would be a grave mistake. And I do mean grave."

"All you gotta do is sell us the place for five thousand dollars, and nothin' bad happens," Jake interjected. "And we're patient men. We'll give you a day or two to think our offer over. Believe me, you'll be plenty sorry if you turn us down."

Nancy's hand went to her mouth, and she suddenly looked ten years beyond her thirty-nine. Her husband put his arm around her and pulled her close as tears spilled down her cheeks.

"Remember," Bud said icily, "if you tell Long Shadow or anyone else about this visit, I promise you'll never have any grandchildren."

Leaving a stunned and weeping couple, the Curry brothers mounted up and rode away. The ranch buildings had barely passed from view, and they were rowdily congratulating themselves on their victory, when Jake pointed across a field and said, "Hey, look! That guy ridin' alone out there looks like Furman's kid."

Eager to terrorize the family even more, Bud chuckled. "He'll pass that brush over there in a few minutes. Let's hide in it and jump him from behind when he does. We'll give him somethin' that'll help make up his parents' mind about sellin'."

Stashing their horses, the brothers hunkered low in the brush as an unsuspecting seventeen-year-old Danny Furman guided his horse steadily toward them.

Bud gripped his rifle and whispered, "You guys stay here. I'm tallest, so I'll get better leverage." Waiting until the youth had passed their hiding spot, the eldest brother silently ran up behind him and swung the weapon. The butt connected violently with Danny's head, and he peeled out of the saddle and hit the ground. The horse trotted away a short distance and stopped.

Bud stood over young Furman as his brothers came out of the brush, and when they drew up, he told them, "He's out cold. Never knew what hit him."

Bending over, Jake examined the youth and said, "You split the skin. He's bleedin'."

"He'll live," Bud retorted. As they headed back for their horses, he laughed and said, "When the kid gets home with that bloody knot on his head, his old man'll get the message. If we can knock the kid out, we can also kill him."

The marshal of Cheyenne Crossing was in his office, cleaning out a desk drawer, when he heard someone step through the open doorway. Looking up, he saw Sally Tottingham silhouetted against the brilliance of the sun-washed street behind her. "Hello, Sally," he said, rising to his feet. As she took a couple of steps inside and he could see her face clearly, he read the worry in her eyes. "What's the matter?" he asked.

"It's Danny Furman, Long Shadow," she replied, her voice shaky. "Mel and Nancy just brought him to the clinic. He was riding alone earlier today, returning home from a neighboring ranch, and somebody hit him on the head from behind and left him lying there. A couple of neighbors found him. Ron is working on him but says he may die. I thought you might want to come talk to his parents."

Long Shadow was already rounding the desk with his hat in his hand. Mumbling indistinctly, he took her arm and ushered her through the door.

Sally had to almost run to keep up with the tall Indian's long, swift strides. Breathing hard, she asked, "What did you say?"

"I said *Curry*. I know as sure as I know my own
name that Abner Curry and his sons are involved in
what happened to Danny. Is the boy conscious?"

"No. He came to long enough for Ron to ask him if
he knew who hit him, and Danny said he never saw his
assailant. Then he blacked out again."

"Did Mel say if any of the Currys had been at his
place before this happened?"

"No."

"I'd bet my last dollar they were."

Entering the clinic, Long Shadow nodded to Danny's
sisters seated in the waiting room, then hurried into the
operating room and found the doctor working feverishly
on the youth. The Furmans stood watching Ronald
Tottingham, worry and strain showing on their faces,
and Tottingham's own face was grim as he told Long
Shadow the youth had been hit savagely on the back of
the head with a blunt instrument, probably the barrel
or butt of a rifle or gun.

The lawman turned to the Furmans, who clung to
each other for support, and asked, "Do you have any
idea who did this to your boy?"

The rancher and his wife looked intently at each
other for a long moment. Then Furman glanced at the
marshal, not meeting his eyes, and quietly replied,
"We have no idea at all."

Long Shadow saw the trepidation in their faces and
sensed that the Furmans were afraid to tell the truth:
They had been visited and threatened by the Currys.
Not wanting to push the issue, he asked Furman to
describe where Danny had been found so that he might
look the area over to possibly find a clue to the assailant's identity. Receiving the information, he left, saying
he would return later.

At sunset, after a comprehensive search that yielded

nothing that could incriminate any of the Currys, Long Shadow returned to town, checked in at the clinic, then headed home for supper. He then returned to the clinic, where both Sally and Ron Tottingham labored into the night. Finally Danny Furman regained consciousness, and Tottingham was able to tell the Furmans and the marshal that the youth would be all right. Greatly relieved, the parents took their weary girls home. Long Shadow also headed for home, with anger toward the Currys smoldering hot within him.

Early the next morning Long Shadow rode to the Furman ranch, and when Mel Furman answered the lawman's knock and saw the towering marshal on the porch, his face blanched and he asked shakily, "Is something wrong with Danny, Marshal?"

"No, it's nothing like that," Long Shadow replied quickly. "In fact, I stopped by the clinic before leaving to come here, and he's doing quite well. He was sitting up and taking nourishment from Sally."

"Could I offer you some coffee, Marshal?" asked Nancy, who had joined her husband at the door.

"Thank you, but I really don't have time. I need to speak with Mel privately."

Furman and his wife exchanged a wordless glance, and then he looked at the marshal. "Sure," he responded. "I was just about finished with breakfast, anyway. Let's take a walk."

The men strolled toward the barn and corral, and when Long Shadow knew they were out of earshot of the house, he said, "Mel, I've got a strong feeling that you know who hit Danny in the head. Will you shoot square with me?"

They stepped around the barn, putting the house out

of sight. Stopping, the rancher looked the taller man in the eye and replied, "Sure."

Holding the smaller man's gaze, the marshal asked, "It was the Currys, wasn't it?"

Furman dropped his eyes and rubbed the back of his neck nervously. "I . . . don't know, Marshal. Why . . . why would you think the Currys might do such a thing?"

"Come on, Mel," Long Shadow said in a tone of frustration. "You know what's been happening in this valley. People have been moving out, leaving Abner Curry holding the mortgage to their properties. That skunk and his sons are using extortion to gobble up land in this valley, but they're so slick and vicious that I can't get the goods on them. They've got people so scared that no one will come forward and tell the truth so I can arrest the Currys."

Furman still did not look up. Staring at the man's bent head, Long Shadow said, "You're scared, Mel, and I know why. Some of the Currys were here yesterday, trying to force you to sell your place to them for a dirt-cheap price, but you refused, so they threatened your family and then gave you time to think it over. No doubt they happened upon Danny after they left here and figured to impress you that they aren't playing games by bashing him in the head. Is that the way it happened."

Still looking down, Furman rubbed his neck again and replied, "No, Marshal. Nothing like that happened at all. You've got it all wrong."

"Mel, you and I have known each other a long time, and you've always looked me in the eye. But you won't look me in the eye right now because you're not being truthful."

Furman did not respond.

Long Shadow reached out and squeezed the rancher's shoulder. "Look, if you'll tell me the truth and press charges against the Currys for extortion, I can lock them up today. Your testimony of what happened here yesterday, along with Nancy's and what happened to Danny, will carry a lot of weight in a courtroom. And if nothing else, it might scare Abner and his no-good sons into giving up their nefarious scheme."

Lifting his head, Furman met Long Shadow's gaze, and it was obvious that he was terrified. "Let's say you were right in your assumption, Marshal. If our testimony and what happened to Danny isn't enough to convince a judge and jury that the Currys are guilty, instead of being in prison, they'd be free to carry out their evil threats. Then my family would be vulnerable to whatever the Currys wanted to do. So it's like I told you. I have no idea who attacked my son."

Abner Curry and his four sons were leaning on the pole fence at their corral, along with several of the ranch hands, and all the men were yelling encouragement to a bronc buster who was riding a spirited horse, breaking it to the saddle. Emmett Curry happened to turn and look toward the house, and when he saw the white hat and buckskin shirt of the approaching rider, he elbowed his father and muttered, "More trouble, Pa."

Abner's head jerked around. Seeing the marshal, he swore and said quietly, "I don't want to talk to him with the men close by." Motioning to his other sons, the elder Curry led them back to the house. When Long Shadow drew up, Abner glared at the marshal with a disgusted look on his face and announced, "If you want to talk, let's do it up on the porch."

The marshal dismounted and followed the five men up the steps. Abner then pivoted, faced Long Shadow, and snapped, "Okay, what is it this time?"

"Danny Furman," came the cold, level reply.

Bud, Jake, and Reese had told their father about their attack on Danny Furman, and the patriarch had spoken his approval. Playing ignorant, he said, "Danny Furman . . . who's he? Oh, wait a minute. Ain't he Mel Furman's kid?"

"I'm not going to play games with you, Curry," Long Shadow retorted. "The boy almost died. If he had, I'd be after you for murder. I can't get Mel to tell me which of your bunch was at his place yesterday, or even to admit he had a visit, but sooner or later I'm going to catch you underhanded scum at your own game, and you'll all go to prison for extortion."

Defiance leapt into Abner Curry's wide-set eyes, and he said with a laugh, "You're barkin' up a tree, *Indian dog*, but there ain't no possum up there. We ain't botherin' nobody, and you can't prove otherwise. The folks who sold us their ranches did so because they were wantin' to leave these parts. I don't know what happened to Furman's kid, but don't try to pin it on me or my boys." His voice turned colder as he added, "Now, I'll thank you to leave my ranch."

Long Shadow glared at the Curry men, then hurried to his horse and mounted. Before riding away, he looked the elder Curry in the eye, declaring, "I'm going to nail you and those four culprits standing with you. If you're a gambler, bet on it, for it's a sure thing."

When the marshal was gone, Reese Curry spit on the ground and grumbled, "He's got to die, Pa. Let's saddle up right now, ride a circle around him, and ambush him. We can fill him so full of lead it'll take a dozen pallbearers to carry his coffin."

Abner vigorously shook his head. "No! I keep tellin' you he's got ways of savin' his skin and stayin' alive— and I don't want any of you doin' somethin' that might endanger you. You boys are my whole life, and I love you."

Clearly touched by his father's sudden tenderness, Emmett put an arm around Abner's shoulder, saying, "I love you, too, Pa."

The gruff rancher glanced up at his youngest—and favorite—son while the others looked on silently. They had always attributed Abner's favoritism to their mother having died giving birth to Emmett, for it seemed as though Abner felt closer to her through Emmett.

After supper that night, Reese and Bud told their father they were going into town to play poker at the Pine Tree Saloon. But Reese slipped out of the house carrying a double-barreled shotgun, for the brothers had decided that the marshal, who was so close to his family, needed a little scare himself.

Just before the children's bedtime, Long Shadow and Little Sun were wrestling in the middle of the parlor floor, while April Dawn and Star Light watched with delight.

As the two males grunted and grappled energetically, Long Shadow allowed his son to pin him down. Laughing victoriously, the boy lay over his father's chest, believing he had him in a hold from which he could not escape.

"Now what are you going to do, Papa?" the boy crowed.

"This!" Long Shadow replied with a laugh, tickling his son in the ribs.

While his mother and sister pealed with laughter, Little Sun giggled and let go of his father, trying to remove the hands that were tickling him. Suddenly the mirth was interrupted by the blast of a shotgun that took out the window, ripping the curtains and burying buckshot in a wall.

"Get down!" Long Shadow screamed at April Dawn and Star Light, who were already dropping to the floor.

The lawman gripped his son and dragged him across the floor to his wife and daughter. He then flattened them and threw his body over them as a shield while rapid rifle fire exploded from outside. Bullets chewed into the house, shattering an adjacent window and showering the occupants with broken glass and splintered wood.

The gunfire stopped as abruptly as it had started. Telling his family to stay down, Long Shadow grabbed his revolver from the table where he had left it before the wrestling match and dashed to the door. He opened it cautiously and heard the sound of galloping hooves quickly diminishing. "All right," he called to the others, "you can get up. They're gone."

April Dawn was trying to comfort Star Light, who was whimpering with fright, as the three of them made their way to where Long Shadow stood. There were splinters in their hair and on their clothing, along with shiny bits of broken glass. Looking them over quickly, Long Shadow asked, "Everybody all right?"

Sniffling, the little girl assured her father she was not hurt, and April Dawn and Little Sun answered similarly.

His face filled with rage, Long Shadow growled, "I'm going to saddle up and ride like the wind to the Curry place. If I find any sweating horses there, somebody's going to get arrested."

Racing outside, the lawman found the corral gate standing open, and he immediately knew the four family horses were gone. A quick check inside the barn confirmed his suspicions.

Returning to the house, Long Shadow told April

Dawn that the horses were gone, no doubt let out before the Currys opened fire, and he would have to hunt them down.

It took him nearly an hour to round up the horses, which he had found scattered about town, and it was then too late to ride to the Curry ranch. Their horses would be cooled off by now. Closing the corral gate behind the animals, Long Shadow entered the house to find April Dawn cleaning up the parlor and the children in bed. The lawman took his wife into his arms, kissed her warmly, then held her tight.

After a few moments April Dawn pulled her head away and looked into his face.

The black-haired beauty said softly, "Your eyes burn with fury—even more so than when Reese Curry kissed me and slapped Little Sun."

"Shotguns and rifles are far more damaging than lips and palms. Those filthy beasts could have killed you or the children." His breath grew hotter and his voice sounded dangerous as he growled through his teeth, "They would dare to do this to my family!"

# Chapter Six

**A**bner Curry tossed and turned in his bed all night. When Bud and Reese had come home just before he went to bed and told him what they had done, he exploded in anger at their foolhardiness. But when Bud explained that the interfering marshal needed a scare to keep him off balance, Abner finally agreed that the idea was a good one after all . . . except that they would certainly get another visit from Long Shadow, and the lawman was going to be red-hot.

Thoughts of that potential visit and the inevitable confrontation that would result kept the elder Curry from getting a decent night's sleep. It was not that he was afraid of the Indian; it was more a matter of his grand scheme being threatened. He had worked at it too long and things had gone too far for him to see his plan destroyed now.

At first light he rose and hurriedly shaved. Going to the kitchen, he built a fire and started making coffee. His task was interrupted by a loud pounding at the front door of the house. Knowing who it was, Abner stalked through the hall to the front door and, steeling himself, pulled it open.

By now he was used to seeing the Indian lawman angry, but he was not prepared for the degree of rage that was written on Long Shadow's face. Covering his surprise, Abner snapped, "What do you want at this hour?"

The Cheyenne's lips were drawn so tight they appeared bloodless. "How many of your boys did you send to shoot up my house last night?" he snarled.

Feigning shock, Abner arched his eyebrows and asked, "Somebody shot up your house? I hope no one was hurt. Even though I don't like stinkin' redskins, I wouldn't want your wife or kids to be injured."

"You're a poor actor, Curry," Long Shadow rasped. "Who did you send? Bud, Reese, and Jake? I doubt you'd let Emmett in on it. He might have ended up with a skinned knee or something."

Abner's eyes glinted. "You're barkin' up a tree again, Indian hound. My boys were home with me all evening."

"You're a liar, Curry!" the lawman countered.

There was an abrupt sound of shuffling feet and a babel of sleep-filled voices as the four Curry brothers came down the hallway. Their hair was disheveled and their eyes were droopy from just being awakened.

As the foursome entered the kitchen and saw the lawman, Bud demanded, "Now what?"

"Well, boys, the marshal says somebody shot up his house last night," the elder Curry replied. "Seems he thinks I sent you to do it."

Bud rubbed his eyes and said, "Guess you'll have to go accuse somebody else, lawman, 'cause we were home all evenin'."

"What'd I tell you?" Abner asked rhetorically. "Maybe you'd like to ask my housekeeper when she wakes up. Or ask a couple of the men in the bunkhouse."

"You no doubt have trained them to lie, too," the Indian said with disgust. Glaring at the five of them, he spat, "You mangy animals could have killed my family!

I'm warning you: You're playing with fire, and you're going to get burned!"

Reese touched his still-battered face, and his voice was bitter as he said, "Let's see you prove it was any of us who shot up your house, Marshal."

"I can't, but you're guilty as sin, and everyone in this room knows it. I just want all of you to understand that nobody touches my family and gets away with it. Your day is coming. That's a promise."

With that, Long Shadow wheeled and strode toward the front of the house. The Curry clan followed him outside, watching from the porch as the lawman vaulted onto his horse and rode off.

Abner Curry stared after the Indian until he was no longer visible. His sons flanked him on both sides, waiting for him to speak, and the patriarch finally remarked, "He can howl all he wants, but without proof, he's barkin' up an empty tree." He paused, then instructed, "Bud, take Jake and Reese to pay a visit on Darrell Brown. Scare him good. Be careful—but be tough. Real tough. I want you comin' back with the good news that he's eager to sell as soon as possible."

Marshal Long Shadow was looking through some wanted posters when the door to his office opened and Cheyenne Crossing's attorney, Todd Bannister, entered.

Bannister, a man of medium build in his early forties, said, "Marshal, a moment of your time, if you're not too busy."

Motioning to the chair in front of his desk, Long Shadow responded, "Not at all. What is it, Todd?"

Bannister sat and took off his hat, resting it on his knee. With a sigh, he replied, "It's Darrell Brown. He's agreed to sell his ranch to Abner Curry."

Long Shadow's face clouded. "When did this happen?"

"Earlier this morning. Darrell came to my house and

told me he's decided to sell out and move to Wyoming
somewhere. Wanted me to draw up the papers. He's
selling for peanuts, Marshal. I pointed this out to him,
but he said it was all he needed for the place. It's
absurd! The man's got nine hundred acres, and he's
letting Curry have it for six thousand dollars. It's worth
four times that. Maybe more. He just built a big new
barn."

Long Shadow's dark skin mottled with anger. Teeth
clenched, he fumed, "You and I both know what's
going on."

"Yeah," the attorney agreed, nodding, "but Darrell's
too frightened to admit it. I drew up the papers and
then rode back with him to his place, on my way to the
Curry ranch. I stopped long enough to say hello to
Roberta, and she looked like a rabbit cornered by a fox.
Pale as a ghost, she was. When I asked her about it, she
passed it off by saying she hasn't been feeling well for
several days."

Long Shadow slammed the desktop with his fist.
"Those blasted Currys! So what's the status at this
moment? You said Darrell's agreed to sell. Does that
mean the papers haven't been signed yet?"

"Not yet. Abner has them right now. He wanted to
look them over—to make sure everything was worded
to his satisfaction. He and Darrell are supposed to meet
at my office tomorrow morning to transfer the deed,
and the money will be exchanged at that time. The
Browns and their four children will be leaving the
valley within a week."

The marshal sprang to his feet. "I'm going to put a
stop to the sale before it happens," he growled. "Thanks
for letting me know."

Less than an hour later, Long Shadow was seated at
the Browns' kitchen table opposite the nervous couple.

Looking earnestly into each of their faces, the lawman told them, "If you'll just tell me the truth, I can throw the Currys in jail for extortion. Todd tells me your place is worth at least four times what you're accepting for it, so I have no doubt they've threatened harm to you and your children. I promise that if you press charges for the threats, I can make them stick in court. And if you folks will do it, other extorted families will find the courage to come forward. A courtroom full of witnesses will put the Currys behind bars for a good long time. But somebody has to be first. Will you do it, Darrell? I can't touch those crooks without your help."

Darrell Brown's voice was fearful as he held Roberta's trembling hand and responded, "It just isn't what you think, Marshal. We've been talking about moving to Wyoming for some time. There's great ranchland over there, and—"

"Just how long have you been talking about it?" Long Shadow cut in. "Since the Currys came to visit you yesterday?"

Brown bit his lip. Shaking his head, he answered, "I tell you, they didn't make any threats. They only came to make the offer because they heard we were thinking about going to Wyoming."

Long Shadow sat back in the chair and scrubbed a palm over his face. "You're not a very good liar, Darrell." Swinging his hard gaze to the woman, he said, "He *is* lying, isn't he, Roberta?"

The rancher's wife turned her head away. When she began to cry, Brown reluctantly confessed, "Okay, Marshal, I lied. But I refuse to implicate the Currys. They're vicious, and they'll go to any lengths to get what they want. It isn't worth getting my family maimed or killed to stay here."

"But if you'll press charges, I can jail them. They can't maim or kill anyone locked up in a cell."

Brown stared at the lawman for a long moment, obviously contemplating his words. Then fear took over, and he shook his head. "I can't do it, Marshal. It's too risky."

"Please," Long Shadow begged. "The Currys can be whipped if just one of their victims refuses to cower and presses charges." Pausing for effect, he then suggested, "Let's you and I ride over to Curry's place right now and tell Abner the deal is off—and you're pressing charges. I'll arrest the whole bunch on the spot and throw them in jail."

A whimper at the other end of the kitchen drew Darrell's attention. His two oldest children, nine-year-old Kyle and seven-year-old Kenton, were standing in the doorway, terror written on their young faces.

Frowning, the rancher asked, "How long have you boys been standing there?"

"Just a little while," Kyle answered timidly. "Are those mean-looking men who were here yesterday going to take our ranch away from us, Daddy?"

Brown looked at his wife, who was biting her lip, then swung his gaze to the marshal. Running a shaky hand through his hair, he said, "Marshal, I can't press charges. It's just too dangerous."

Long Shadow sighed. "Will you at least refuse to sell?"

Brown looked back at his boys.

"We don't want to move away, Daddy," Kyle said sadly.

Roberta touched her husband's arm. "Let's call off the sale, Darrell. Ride to the Curry ranch with Marshal Long Shadow and tell those beasts we're staying. When they see that you aren't pressing charges, maybe they'll leave us alone."

Taking the hand that was on his arm, Brown squeezed it and said, "We'll let Curry know we're backing out on the sale, honey, but I'm not leaving you and the children here alone."

"Tell you what, Darrell," the Indian spoke up, "I'll go break the news for you. I wish you'd press charges, but at least there's a partial victory here. Those greedy dogs won't get your ranch."

Riding up to the Curry house, Long Shadow dismounted and roughly asked Emmett Curry, who was sitting alone on the porch, "Where's your father?"

The youngest Curry got to his feet and gave the lawman a bland look, finally replying, "In his den with Reese. But he don't want to see you."

"I want to see *him*! Lead me there," Long Shadow ordered as he climbed the porch steps. The two men were exactly the same height, and the lawman's black eyes narrowed and bored into the youth's. "Now."

Emmett led the marshal through the house to the den. Abner was seated behind a large, ornate oak desk and Reese lounged in a wing chair beside the desk. At the sight of the lawman both men became visibly irritated.

"What now?" Abner blurted.

Long Shadow strode to the desk, looked down at the beefy senior Curry and announced, "I've got some bad news for you. You're not getting the Brown ranch."

All the color seeped out of the elder man's face. His eyes bulging, he demanded, "What're you talkin' about?"

Reese raised his stocky frame out of the chair and stepped behind it, alongside Emmett, as Long Shadow replied, "Darrell Brown sent me here to tell you the sale is off."

"Why didn't he come himself?" Abner fumed.

"He has other things to do. I volunteered to run this little errand for him."

Slamming the desk with his fist, the thick-bodied rancher swore vehemently, then stood up. Wrath gushed out of him like water bursting from a broken dam. "You rotten redskin!" he bellowed. "That badge don't give you the right to stick your nose into my business! You're overextendin' your bounds!" Picking up the newly written deed, he snarled, "This is a legal transaction that you have no right to interfere with!"

Long Shadow snatched the papers from Curry's grasp and ripped them to shreds, then announced through clenched teeth, "There *is* no transaction anymore, mister!"

From the corner of his eye, Long Shadow saw Reese claw for the revolver on his hip. In a flash the marshal's gun was out and cocked; at the same instant Abner roared, "*Reese, no!*"

The young rancher's hand froze with his gun halfway out of its holster.

Holding the ominous muzzle pointed at Reese's chest, Long Shadow told him, "You were within a heartbeat of dying."

Abner licked his lips and said quietly, "That was a foolish move, son. I've told you not to try to match fists or guns with this blasted redskin."

Reese eyed his father, then holstered his gun. When Long Shadow did the same with his Colt .45, the husky young Curry glared hotly at the lawman and growled, "I'm sick and tired of you harassin' us! Every time we turn around, you're accusin' us of somethin', and all the while we're innocent! If you had anythin' to arrest us for, you'd do it, but you don't, so get off our property!"

"Innocent," Long Shadow spat, as if the word burned

his tongue. "You and your family don't know what that word means! One of these days you'll threaten the wrong rancher, one who's got enough guts to press charges. Then I'm going to arrest all of you, leaving you to rot in prison." Dropping the bits of paper onto the floor like so many fallen autumn leaves, Long Shadow stormed out of the room and bolted from the house.

Ranch hand Jack Burt, a stringy cowboy in his late twenties, was just stepping up onto the porch, and he moved aside to let the lawman pass. While he stood watching Long Shadow ride away, Burt heard the Currys cursing the Indian.

Knocking on the frame of the open door, Burt called, "Mr. Curry, it's Jack! Can I come in?"

"Yeah, Jack! Come on in!"

When Burt entered the den, Emmett was on his knees picking up the torn papers while Reese stalked around the room cursing, and Abner sat behind his desk fuming. Seeing the cowhand, the patriarch cautioned his son to be quiet, but Burt assured him, "It's all right, Mr. Curry. Me and the rest of the fellas, we all know about the marshal tryin' to pin extortion charges on you and your sons. Heck, it's all over the valley."

Lighting a cigarette, Abner replied, "I should have known you'd hear about it. Any of the men seem inclined to quit because of it?"

"None that I know of, sir. You pay us better'n we've ever been paid before. We're stickin' with you."

"Good," Abner responded smugly, blowing smoke toward the beamed ceiling. "What did you want to see me about, Jack?"

"We finished that stretch of fence you had us repairin'. You want us to work on that other stretch over by the creek?"

"Yeah. There's about eighty feet of it in bad shape. Set new posts and use new wire."

"Will do," Burt confirmed and turned to leave. Reaching the door, he stopped, pivoted, and said, "Mr. Curry . . ."

"Yeah?"

"I agree with your feelin's about that stinkin' redskin. Seems like somebody oughta plug that thorn in your side. He wouldn't be any problem if he was six feet under."

Spitting tobacco off his tongue, Abner responded, "A lot of men have tried to bury him—some of 'em expert gunfighters. But facin' him or comin' up on his back, they haven't been able to do it. *They're* the ones who are six feet under, and that redskin lives on. No, forget that the thought ever came to your mind."

Burt left the house and approached a group of ranch hands waiting for him near the toolshed. After instructing them on their chore, he told them, "I'll see you later. I have somethin' else to do."

Hurrying into the barn, Burt saddled his horse and led it into the corral. He checked the loads in his Winchester .44, shoved it into the saddleboot, then leapt into the saddle and galloped toward town.

Jack Burt's heart pounded in his chest as the warm wind brushed his face. He would ambush the marshal, kill him, and bring his body to Abner Curry. By removing the troublesome lawman from Curry's path, Burt would rise in stature in the boss's eyes. The deed would no doubt gain him a nice financial bonus, too.

Lashing his horse, Burt rode hard until he caught sight of Long Shadow about a half mile ahead of him on the open plain, moving at a medium trot and about to enter the forest. The cowboy pushed his mount even harder and made a circle around the edge of the timber in order to get ahead of his prey, knowing the path Long Shadow would take through the forest to reach Cheyenne Crossing. When Burt was satisfied he had found a good spot to work his ambush, he jerked his horse to a halt and stashed the sweating, panting animal behind a rock outcropping. Grabbing his rifle, he positioned himself in a thicket beside the path.

Burt knew he had gained considerably on the marshal and had several minutes yet, so he sat and waited. A large flock of blackbirds appeared overhead, squawking as they circled above the forest. After a moment, they descended onto the branches of the trees that surrounded him.

The would-be killer sat listening to the chatter of the birds while keeping a steady eye on the path through the branches of the thicket. Soon he heard the dull clopping of hooves on the forest floor, and his nerves tightened. Suddenly Long Shadow came into view, no more than thirty yards away. Burt quickly got to his knees, worked the lever of the rifle, and took aim. But his abrupt movement and the clicking sound disturbed the blackbirds overhead.

Long Shadow, like all Indians, had a special affinity with nature, and he was in tune with the rhythm of the forest. He could listen to the chatter of squirrels and other small creatures of the forest and know when a storm was coming. He could sense the mood of wild animals when danger lurked close by.

Trotting through the forest, he heard the loud squawking of blackbirds up ahead, and the tone told him that the birds had been frightened. His forehead furrowed, and his instincts caused him to draw back on the reins as a black swarm lifted from the trees just ahead on the path. It was warning enough for the Cheyenne. As he dived from the saddle he heard the rifle crack. The bullet chewed into a tree close by, and his horse whinnied as it wheeled and galloped several yards back the way it had come.

Taking refuge behind a tree, Long Shadow pulled his Colt .45 and peered around the trunk, trying to locate his assailant. The man gave away his position when he cursed violently at having missed the lawman; then the oath was followed by another crack of the rifle, and a slug chewed into the bark just above the marshal's head. Spotting his would-be assassin, Long Shadow fired, and Jack Burt was felled by a .45-caliber slug exploding his heart.

Long Shadow holstered his gun and walked over to the thicket. Parting it, he looked down at the dead man's face and quickly recognized him as the cowboy he had passed on the Curry porch, and anger coursed through his body like lava.

Abner Curry looked up from his desk as his youngest son bolted into the den, gasping, "Pa, that Indian marshal is comin' back!"

"Again?" Abner shouted, slamming down the pencil in his hand. "I'm gettin' sick and tired of—"

"He's leadin' a horse with a body draped over it," Emmett interjected.

Rising to his feet, Abner asked, "You recognize the horse?"

"I think it's Jack's."

Muttering, the rancher rounded the desk and hurried to the front porch. As Long Shadow came closer, Abner stood aghast at the sight of the lanky body draped over the horse's saddle.

The marshal's face was grim and hard as he hauled up. "Your plan didn't work, Curry," he snarled.

Shaking his head, Abner protested, "I know what it looks like, Marshal, but it ain't so."

"Why just one man?" the lawman scoffed. "You must have twenty hands on your payroll. That many would probably have gotten the job done."

Abner Curry's face hardened as he blustered, "I didn't send him to kill you, Long Shadow! That's the honest truth!"

Dropping the reins of Burt's horse in the dust, the Indian regarded the man with contempt and retorted, "You wouldn't know the honest truth if it jumped up and bit the end of your lying tongue off." Turning his horse around, Long Shadow added over his shoulder, "Just keep it up, Curry. I'll get you."

# Chapter Seven

**B**right morning sun shone down on Kyle and Kenton Brown as they ran out of the house, leaving their two younger siblings inside with their mother. They raced over to the corral, where their father was installing hinges on the corral gate next to the new barn.

The boys approached their father, and Kyle asked, "Daddy, when are we going to town?"

"As soon as I finish with this gate, son," Brown replied gently. "You boys go on and play now, and let me get it done."

"Can we help you hitch the horses to the wagon, Daddy?" Kenton asked.

"When I get ready to do it, you certainly can," Brown assured the boy with a smile. "Don't stray off too far. As soon as I'm finished here and I put the tools away, I'll call you."

The brothers skipped away and, unnoticed by their father, entered the new barn. They decided to play in the hayloft, so when their father came into the barn to put the tools away, they would see him and be ready to leave. Giggling, they climbed the ladder and began to wrestle in the hay.

After exhausting themselves by playing hard for some twenty minutes, they lay back in the hay, catching their breath. Suddenly the rear door of the barn squeaked open, and they quickly sat up. They could still hear their father working at the front of the barn, and they knew their mother was in the house with their brothers. Who could be coming into the barn from out back?

Kyle put a forefinger to his lips, warning his younger brother to be quiet, and they cautiously crawled to the edge of the loft and looked down. The sight of the two men entering the barn made their eyes bulge, and as they eased back into the hay, Kyle whispered, "It's those mean men who were here day before yesterday to take our ranch away from us!"

Kenton whispered, "Let's call Daddy!"

"No!" Kyle breathed. "They've got guns! They'll shoot us! Be real still!"

Bud and Reese Curry crept into the barn, pulling the door closed behind them, and slowly made their way toward the partly open front door. Bud reached it first, and peered through the opening. Whirling about, he cautioned, "He's comin'! Move back into the shadows!"

Darrell Brown swung the big door wider and entered the barn, carrying his tools. Watching in terror from the loft, Kyle and Kenton hardly breathed as the rancher entered the small room that was off to one side, hung up his tools, and started back into the main room. Suddenly he stopped and looked into the shadows beneath the hayloft, then stiffened as the Curry brothers stepped into the light.

"What do you want?" Brown demanded angrily.

Halting a few feet from him, the brothers glanced at each other. Then Bud fixed hard eyes on the rancher and answered, "We came to tell you our pa is mighty sore at you for backin' out on the deal."

"But we're reasonable men, Brown," Reese added, fingering his scabs. "We're givin' you a chance to realize that you'd best reconsider and sell."

Having been encouraged by Marshal Long Shadow's help in the matter, Brown was feeling less intimidated by the Currys. Squaring his shoulders and raising his chin, the rancher replied stiffly, "There's not going to be any sale, so get on your horses and ride. Coming here was a waste of time."

"You're makin' a big mistake, mister!" Reese blared. "That stinkin' redskin marshal ain't here to protect you, and if we don't hear right now that the deal is back on, you're gonna be plenty sorry!"

But Brown loudly retorted, "You people already own more land in this valley than anyone else! Isn't that enough for you? Get out of here and leave me alone!"

Reese's fleshy face reddened. Taking a step closer and raising his fist threateningly, he shouted, "We offered you a fair price for this place, and you've got ten seconds to change your mind and sell!"

Adamant, the rancher gestured toward the big door, and his harsh voice rang through the barn as he snapped, "Get out of here! You'll regret coming onto my land and threatening me! Go on, get out!"

Backing up his brother, Bud shook his head and hissed, "You're a fool, Brown. You can't win against us."

"With the help of the law I can," the rancher countered. "Marshal Long Shadow is just waiting for the chance to nail you crooks. If you pull anything here, he'll have you!"

A menacing, cruel smile on his face, Bud retorted, "Like Reese said, your marshal friend ain't here to help you. I think you need some further persuadin', so my brother's gonna go into the house. By the time he's through beatin' your wife and kids, I think you'll see fit to change your mind."

Pushed beyond his limit, his instinct to protect his family stronger than his reason, Darrell Brown whirled and grabbed a pitchfork that was leaning against the wall. As he came around with it, Bud and Reese pulled their guns and fired.

The two boys in the hayloft watched in dumbstruck horror as their father went down, still gripping the pitchfork, while the gunshots reverberated through the barn.

Quickly the Curry brothers darted out the rear door of the barn, ran across the corral, and leapt over the fence. Vaulting into their saddles, they spurred their mounts and galloped off, plunging into the dense forest seconds later and vanishing from sight.

Inside the barn, Kyle and Kenton scurried down the ladder, sobbing and crying, "Daddy! Daddy!" As they reached the murdered rancher, they could hear their mother coming on the run, anxiously calling out their father's name.

Bud and Reese Curry were sitting at a table in the Rusty Lantern Saloon. It was early afternoon and the place, which was well occupied with customers, smelled of whiskey, tobacco, smoke, and sweaty bodies.

Looking around to make sure he could not be overheard, Reese asked his older brother, "You think Pa will be mad at us for killin' Brown?"

"Don't know why he should," Bud replied, a cigarette dangling from the corner of his mouth. "We had to defend ourselves against that pitchfork, didn't we?" Blinking against the smoke, he added, "Besides, the new widow ain't gonna be able to run that ranch by herself—which means the place'll be for sale right soon. All we have to do is sit tight for a few days, then pay her a little visit. Our offer will look mighty good by then. Pa'll be proud of us for gettin' the job done."

"Guess you're right," Reese mused. "Since no one saw us on the Brown place, ain't no way the law can connect us with his killin'."

Bud took the cigarette from his mouth and downed the contents of his whiskey glass. Nodding, he responded, "Yeah, but you can bet your boots that redskin'll do his best to nail us anyway."

"Well, he'll be barkin' up an empty tree once again. Let him come."

The Curry brothers were quiet for a few minutes, and then Bud suggested, "We'll swing by the Potter place on the way home. Clarence just might be in the mood to sell the ranch by now. He may miss his old lady, but I bet he ain't eager to join her."

Reese swallowed a mouthful of whiskey, plunked the glass on the table, and laughed. "Yeah. The place is practically ours."

The burly Curry had his back toward the saloon door, and when he noticed his brother's face stiffen, he twisted around in his chair to see what Bud was looking at. Standing in the doorway, silhouetted against the sunlight, was the formidable figure of Marshal Long Shadow. The lawman was running his gaze over the place, apparently looking for someone.

The lawman spotted them and walked to their table. As he towered over the pair, his right hand hung close to his holstered Colt .45. Every eye in the place was on him as he said levelly, "I want both of you to reach down carefully and ease the guns from your holsters. Lay the guns on the table, then stand up."

Bud insolently looked the tall lawman up and down and rasped, "Now, what's this all about?"

Coolly, Long Shadow responded, "You two are under arrest for the murder of Darrell Brown."

The Curry brothers gawked at each other. Recovering, Bud snapped, "We don't know nothin' about any murder. Get off our backs!"

"Ah, but I can't do that," the marshal rejoined. "You see, there were eyewitnesses, and they've identified both of you."

Bud's face paled, as did his brother's. Swallowing hard, he mumbled, "Eyewitnesses?"

"Yep," Long Shadow confirmed, nodding. "I've got their sworn statements, and they'll point you out in court. You went too far this time. Now you're going to hang." He let the words sink in for a few seconds before saying, "I repeat, ease those guns out and lay them on the table."

Rage began to churn inside Reese Curry, and he bellowed, "You're lyin', Indian! You ain't got no eyewitnesses! You're trumpin' this up just so you can put us in jail!"

"I'm not lying," came Long Shadow's calm answer. "I have two witnesses who saw you gun down Darrell Brown, and when the judge and jury see them point you out in the courtroom, your next stop will be the gallows."

Reese's face beaded with sweat as he asked himself who could possibly have seen them. If people had been hiding in the barn, why did they not try to help Brown? Picturing the gallows, the beefy young rancher grew frantic, and he blurted, "You're out of your mind, lawman! There wasn't nobody else inside that barn!"

"Shut up, Reese!" Bud shrieked.

Reese felt a wave of nausea wash over him. By the slip of his tongue, he had just incriminated his brother and himself, even if there were no witnesses.

Cornered, the Curry brothers eyed each other, signaling action. Flipping the table toward Long Shadow, Reese went for his gun, while his brother's revolver was already clearing the holster. The marshal drew and fired with lightning speed, drilling Bud through the heart before patrons even had time to scatter.

Long Shadow swung his smoking Colt on Reese, who was just drawing his revolver. At the sight of the menacing muzzle pointed at his head, he quickly threw the gun to the floor as if it had suddenly turned red-hot. Raising his hands over his head, he begged, "Don't shoot, Marshal! Don't shoot! I give up!"

Gun smoke hung like fog in the saloon as the marshal instructed some of the patrons to carry Bud Curry's body outside and tie it onto his horse. That done, Long Shadow marched Reese to jail and locked him in the cell next to Walt Frick. The outlaw was lying on his bunk, and he sat up when the new prisoner was brought in. Now that Reese was no longer staring at the business end of Long Shadow's gun, his fury resurfaced, and he stood at the bars, swearing at the marshal. The lawman gave him a cold look and, without commenting, left the cellblock.

His departure did nothing to quell the stocky young rancher's rage, and Reese continued to curse and scream, reaching through the bars and shaking his fists. When he finally ran out of steam, he turned to see Frick standing at the bars between the cells.

"I see you feel the same toward that snake-bellied Indian as I do," Frick remarked calmly.

"He just killed my brother!" Reese roared. "I hate his guts!"

"Tell you what," Frick said. "I'm gonna find a way to escape and put as many bullets as I can in those guts. That should please you."

Reese shook the bars and swore again, saying, "You ain't gonna get to kill him, buddy! My pa and my brothers will break me out . . . and when they do, it's gonna be me who kills that Indian scum!"

Staring at the other prisoner with growing anger, Frick told himself there was no way he was going to let someone else have the joy of killing Long Shadow. He wanted that satisfaction for himself. Turning away, he went quietly to his bunk and lay back down.

Outside, Long Shadow stepped into the gun shop next door to tell Barry Hawkins that the deputy would have to watch over the town while he brought Bud Curry's body home. Finding Hawkins's wife behind the counter, he said, "Hello, Rose. Is Barry in the back room?"

"No," the comely woman replied. "Barry's stomach went sour on him just after you got back from the Brown ranch. He went home."

Taking his leave to find someone else to act as deputy, Long Shadow hurried to the Spencer Feed and Grain Company. When he entered the store, he found the tall, graying proprietor, Albert Spencer, writing up a large sale of grain for a local rancher. Both men asked him about the shooting, the news of which was already all over town, and the lawman gave them a brief summary of what happened. He then inquired, "Albert, is Willie here?"

"Yes," Spencer replied. "He's out back. You want me to get him?"

"Yes, but first I need to know if you can spare him for a while. You see, I've got to take Curry's body home, and Barry Hawkins is under the weather. Willie and I have done some target shooting on occasion, so I know he can handle a gun; therefore, I'd like to deputize him so he can stand in for me, if he's willing."

"*If* he's willing?" Spencer said, chuckling. "There'll be no question about that. And you don't need my permission, Marshal. He's twenty-two years old."

"My request for permission was directed to you as his employer, not his father," the marshal said with a smile. "I'll need him to stay at the jail until I get back."

"It's fine with me, Marshal," Spencer assured him. "The work he's doing can wait till tomorrow, if it has to."

Willie Spencer was called from the back room by his father. Tall and lanky, the handsome young man eagerly accepted the marshal's proposition and ran home to get his gun. He promised to meet Long Shadow at his office inside of ten minutes.

Less than fifteen minutes later Long Shadow had deputized Willie Spencer and pinned a badge on his chest. Leading him to the cellblock, he showed the youth the two prisoners, explaining to Frick and Curry that if they had some kind of problem, Willie would be in charge. The lawmen then returned to the office, where Long Shadow briefed the youth on what to do if there was trouble in town. Telling Willie to stay at the jail unless he was called away for an emergency, the marshal left to make his unpleasant visit to the Curry ranch.

In the cellblock, sitting on his bunk, Walt Frick pondered the situation. A green deputy on duty meant the perfect opportunity to escape. His thought was interrupted by Reese Curry's observation. "Now would sure be a good time for my pa and brothers to show up, with that wet-nosed kid in charge."

Frick did not comment. He had to make his escape before the Currys came and rescued Reese. No one was going to kill Long Shadow but Walter P. Frick.

He began pacing back and forth in his cell. Presently Reese took cigarette makings from his pocket, rolling a cigarette while lying on his bunk. When Reese struck a match, an idea clicked in Frick's head, and he stepped to the bars. Looking down at his fellow prisoner, he remarked, "How's about lendin' me some of your tobacco and paper?"

Grudgingly, Reese handed the materials to his neighbor. "Oh, and a match, too," Frick said. Taking the match, he thanked Reese and went to his bunk. Instead of rolling a cigarette, however, he began tearing open his thin mattress.

Reese sat up when he heard cloth ripping. The outlaw glanced at the young rancher but continued with his chore. Frick then tore a strip of bedsheet about a foot wide and a yard long and draped it over his arm.

"What the heck are you doin'?" Curry queried.

"You'll see," Frick replied, grinning, and struck the match on his bunk.

Lighting the exposed feathers, he stood back. Immediately the feathers crackled into flames, sending up clouds of smoke. Then Frick set the strip of cloth afire and held it in front of one leg. Pulling the burning mattress partway off the bunk, he shouted, "Deputy! Hey, Deputy! Fire! Fire!"

The door to the office swung open, and young Willie Spencer appeared. When he saw the smoke and flames, his eyes bulged. Frick stood close to the smoking mattress and held the burning cloth just right, making it appear that his pants were on fire. Jumping up and down, he screamed, "My clothes are burning! Help me!"

Gasping, Willie dashed to the office and returned

quickly, carrying the keys and the water bucket. Frick continued to scream as the deputy set the bucket down and hurriedly unlocked the cell door. Reese Curry caught Frick's eye and smiled, waiting.

Opening the door, Willie took the bucket and ran in, ready to douse the fire. Suddenly Frick threw the burning cloth in the deputy's face, and Willie howled, batting at it and dropping the bucket. The diversion was all the outlaw needed. His meaty fist connected with the deputy's jaw, and the youth bounced off the bars, stunned. Frick punched him again, knocking him out, and Willie sank to the floor.

Grabbing the bucket, Frick put out the fire, then pulled Willie's gun from his holster. From the adjoining cell Reese grinned and exclaimed, "You're a genius, pal! Let's go!"

Shaking his head, Frick stepped out of his cell. "Sorry, friend. You're stayin' here. I told you, *I'm* the guy who's killin' Long Shadow."

Walt Frick bolted through the office door and slammed it, shutting off the sound of Reese Curry's vehement curses.

Emmett Curry sat on the front porch in the late afternoon sun, cleaning his double-barreled .38-caliber derringer, when movement on the grassy prairie caught his attention. Squinting, he could make out a rider leading two horses behind him. Waiting a few moments, he squinted again. This time he could make out the white Stetson worn by Long Shadow and his fringed buckskin shirt.

Emmett's heart leapt to his throat when he recognized Bud's and Reese's horses . . . and saw the lifeless form lying facedown over the saddle of Bud's horse.

Stuffing the derringer in his pocket, Emmett jumped off the porch and bolted toward the barn and corral where his father and Jake were talking to some of the ranch hands. "Pa!" he shouted. "Pa!"

Abner Curry broke off his conversation and turned to watch his favorite son racing toward him. Reaching the corral, Emmett pointed behind him, gasping, "Long Shadow's comin', leadin' Bud's and Reese's horses—and there's a dead man on Bud's horse!"

Feeling dread spread thoughout his body, the patriarch stood immobile, while Jake swore and the cowhands watched in silence. Long Shadow was yet a hundred yards away, but the body on the horse was clearly visible.

With a quiver in his voice, Jake said, "Bud and Reese must have run into trouble at the Brown place, Pa."

Abner Curry was unable to respond. Looking at the body slung over the horse, he felt paralyzed, incapable of speech. He knew that the long, slender body dangling over the saddle was Bud. He wondered where Reese was.

"What should we do, Pa?" Emmett asked, taking hold of his father's arm.

Gritting his teeth, the elder Curry grunted and made a feeble gesture for the ranch hands to leave. Coming to his father's rescue, Jake instructed, "Go on, fellas. This is a family matter."

The men walked away, looking back over their shoulders, and soon entered the bunkhouse.

When Long Shadow reined in, Abner and his two sons gaped at the awful sight for a long moment, not believing their eyes. Finally the rancher rushed to the lifeless form and uttered a wild, mournful wail, and his two sons flanked him helplessly.

Dismounting, Long Shadow stepped behing the three men. Abner was embracing Bud, mumbling incoherently with tears coursing down his cheeks. The elder Curry cradled his dead son's head in his arms for several minutes, crying. Finally, he gently released the body and turned toward the marshal. Hatred flared in his eyes as he grimaced like a mad dog, snarling, "You did this, didn't you?"

Abner and his sons could barely contain themselves as Long Shadow explained all that had happened—from Darrell Brown's murder in front of hidden witnesses to the shooting in the saloon and Reese's being locked up in jail.

When the lawman had finished, the rancher was breathing heavily. Though a storm of wrath and grief raged through the elder Curry, he maintained enough sense to keep himself from making a fatal move against the lawman. His face suffused with blood, and his entire body shook as he clenched his fists and exploded, "You killed my son! *You killed my son!*"

Calmly, Long Shadow said, "It was Bud's own fault that he got killed. He didn't give me a choice. And Reese will stand trial for murder as soon as the circuit judge shows up."

Abner seethed with loathing, his breath sawing in and out of him in hot, angry gasps.

Continuing, Long Shadow said, "I warned you, Curry. Now your extortion scheme has backfired. Bud's dead, and Reese is going to hang. You should have listened to me."

Pivoting, the tall Indian stepped into the stirrup and swung onto his horse. As he rode away, Abner shook his fist at the marshal's back and bawled, "You're wrong, you rotten redskin! Reese is not gonna hang! I promise you that! My boy is not gonna hang!"

Long Shadow did not look back.

Still breathing heavily, Abner turned to his sons and muttered, "The same six men always serve as a jury in Cheyenne Crossing. We've got to get to them before that judge arrives. I won't have any more of my sons taken away from me!"

# Chapter Eight

A hot south wind plucked at Long Shadow's white Stetson as he trotted his horse into Cheyenne Crossing. Lifting the hat momentarily, he sleeved sweat from his brow and his thick black hair. Continuing on, he noticed a small crowd gathered in front of the jail, and in the middle of the crowd, Frank Denton and Willie Spencer were in animated conversation.

Drawing up, the marshal was assailed by a chorus of voices, and he held up his hand and shook his head, not able to understand what anyone was saying. As Long Shadow dismounted, Denton and a miserable-looking Spencer pushed their way through the throng to him. Running his gaze back and forth between the two men, Long Shadow asked, "What's wrong?"

The deputized young man threw up his hands and declared, "It's my fault, Marshal! I let Walt Frick trick me, and he escaped!"

"Escaped!" the Indian gasped. "What about Reese Curry?"

"He's still in there, I'm glad to say," Spencer responded.

"How did Frick do it?"

"Come inside and I'll show you," Spencer said glumly, looking even more hangdog. "I'm really sorry, Marshal. I feel terrible about this."

Denton followed the two men into the marshal's office and down the hallway to the cellblock. Smoke had blackened the back wall of Frick's cell, the partially burned mattress lay on the bunk, and charred feathers and black bits of cloth littered the floor. Reese Curry sat on his bunk, watching them, as the young deputy told the marshal how the outlaw had fooled him into thinking his pants were on fire, lured him into the cell, and knocked him out.

When Spencer had finished, humiliation was in his eyes, and his voice quavered slightly as he said, "Marshal, I feel like such an idiot. I should have been more careful. I should have suspected a trick. If you want me to somehow repay you, I've got it coming."

Towering over him, Long Shadow put a hand on the youth's shoulder. "It's not your fault, Willie. You have no experience in handling criminals. I shouldn't have saddled you with that kind of responsibility. Don't punish yourself. You're not to blame."

Still looking sheepish, Spencer mumbled, "Thanks, Marshal."

Long Shadow stepped to Curry's cell. Looking through the bars, he asked, "I don't suppose you'd tell me if Frick said where he was going."

Reese eyed him sourly. "You're dead right about that, tin star," he replied with loathing.

Long Shadow turned to Willie Spencer and said, "I've got to go after Frick. You still want to wear that badge till I get back?"

The youth smiled broadly. "Yes, sir!"

Looking past him, Long Shadow asked Denton, "You have any objections, Frank?"

"None at all, Marshal. I think Willie can still take care of things for you—and I'd say he's learned about the responsibility that goes with wearing a badge."

"You can say that again, sir!"

Long Shadow looked at Curry, then back at Spencer, telling him, "If Reese's pants catch fire, let him burn. Under no circumstances—and I mean *no* circumstances— are you to open that cell door or even get close to it. Understand?"

"Yes, sir. No matter what he says or does, I won't go near that cell."

Leaving Reese scowling, the three men returned to the office. When the door to the cell area was closed, Long Shadow said, "Willie, I don't think Abner Curry and his bunch would be foolish enough to try to break Reese out of here, but if you should see any of the Currys in town, bolt this door. There's a brand-new shotgun in the gun rack, and if a Curry or anybody who smells like a Curry tries to force his way in, blast him. Got that?"

"Yes, sir."

The lawman and the councilman left the office, and Long Shadow told Denton, "I'm going to ride to the house and let April Dawn know what's happening, and then I'm going after Frick. I have no idea which way he might have gone, but someone is bound to have seen him leaving town. Watch over Willie a little for me, will you?"

"Sure, Marshal," the bank president promised.

After inquiring of several bystanders if any of them had seen Frick and getting no information, Long Shadow was about to mount his horse when the telegrapher dashed out of the Western Union office, waving a yellow piece of paper and calling his name. "What is it, Caleb?" Long Shadow asked the small, elderly man.

"Wire for you, Marshal," the telegrapher replied.

Accepting the yellow sheet, Long Shadow saw that it was signed by a Judge Emery Thorne. He read the message, which explained that Thorne was new to the territory and had recently been appointed to ride the circuit. He was wiring the marshal to let him know that he was in Rapid City and would be coming through Cheyenne Crossing in three days. If there were any court cases pending, he would handle them at that time.

Long Shadow headed home, riding into the warm breeze. Soon the full blast of summer would be upon the Black Hills. Swinging into his yard, he glanced at the house. New glass had been installed in his windows, but bullet holes still pocked the wooden slats near the windows. Then his brow furrowed as he realized that the front door was closed. April Dawn always kept the door open on such pleasant days so fresh air could waft through the screen door. A tiny tingle slithering down Long Shadow's spine alerted him that something was amiss.

Acting as if he suspected nothing, the tall man rode his horse to the rear of the house and dismounted. Glancing casually at the back door as he led the horse to the barn, he noted that it, too, was closed. He knew that even had April Dawn and the children gone shopping, she would have left just the screen doors closed. His sixth sense telling him that something was definitely wrong, he wondered if Walt Frick might have come here seeking revenge. Was Frick now holding his family hostage?

Leading the horse inside the barn, from its shadowy interior the wary lawman observed the rear of the house. A curtain moved at a kitchen window, which meant someone had been watching him. If it was either April Dawn or one of the children, they would now be coming through the door. It had to be Frick!

Long Shadow pulled his revolver, broke it open, and

spun the cylinder, checking the loads. Dropping it back into the holster, he assessed the situation. To enter the house would be extremely dangerous, for it could get his wife or the children killed. It could even get him killed before he could take out Frick. One thing was certain: Frick was out to kill him; there was no question about that.

But he could not leave his family in the hands of the outlaw another minute. He would just have to enter the house acting normal and rely on his skill and experience to gain control.

Flexing the fingers of his gun hand, he lifted the Colt an inch, then let it ease back into place. He crossed the yard at a casual pace, stepped onto the back porch, and turned the knob. His heart was drumming wildly. Pushing the door open, he saw April Dawn seated in the middle of the kitchen floor on a ladder-backed wooden chair, a gag in her mouth and her hands tied behind her back. Her face was pale and stricken. Long Shadow felt a cold wave wash over him, and icy sweat beaded his brow. He wondered where Little Sun and Star Light had been taken.

With her eyes April Dawn informed her husband that the outlaw was in the large pantry just off the kitchen. The door to the pantry was open about an inch, but as the room had no window, Long Shadow saw only darkness.

Suddenly Frick's gravelly voice spewed from the room. "I've got your kids in here with me, Marshal! It ain't them I'm wantin' to hurt, but I'll kill 'em both if you don't do exactly as I say! You got that?"

"I hear you," the tall man replied coldly.

"Good! Now, reach down real slow and take the gun out of the holster with your fingertips. Drop it on the floor, then kick it toward me."

Long Shadow had dealt with criminals for a third of his life. He knew how they thought and most of the time could predict their actions . . . and he was certain that the moment he was no longer armed, Walt Frick would gun him down where he stood. Though he could not see Frick, Long Shadow could tell from his voice exactly where the beefy man was standing, for all that separated the kitchen from the pantry was a thin partition wall. If he could determine where his son and daughter were positioned, he could make his move against the outlaw.

Stalling, he demanded, "I want to know my children are all right."

His words brought muffled squeals from the pantry, and four small feet banged against the floor. He could tell from the source of the sounds that Little Sun and Star Light were on the floor—and that was all Long Shadow needed to know. His gun was out in a split second, firing through the thin wall. He heard Frick grunt and stumble back into the shelves with the first shot, but he would take no chances. The gun roared three more times, placing small black holes in the white wall.

The children squealed again as dishes, pots, pans, and canned goods tumbled from the shelves. Dashing to the pantry, his gun held ready, the anxious father jerked the door open. Walt Frick lay in a grotesque heap under various and sundry items with three bullets in his upper chest and one in his forehead. Long Shadow holstered his weapon and gathered the children into his arms. Moments later April Dawn and the children were freed from their bonds and gags, and the relieved family embraced.

Word of the incident spread quickly through Cheyenne Crossing, confirming the fact that threatening Long

Shadow's family was akin to getting too close to a teased rattler . . . and could be even more dangerous.

Cheyenne Crossing's town hall became a courthouse whenever a circuit judge arrived to hold trials. Judge Emery Thorne appeared as he had promised, and at one o'clock in the afternoon on the day of his arrival, Reese Curry's trial began.

The courtroom was jammed. Abner Curry, his other two sons, and about a dozen of his ranch hands sat on the right side of the room, just behind the table where Reese was seated with the Cheyenne standing beside him. In contrast to the tall lawman, the middle-aged Thorne was short, stocky, and balding, and his tough, jowly face was reminiscent of a bulldog's.

Abner, Jake, and Emmett had been given a few minutes to privately visit Reese at the jail, and to the surprise of the other spectators, the Currys seemed completely at ease as the judge banged his gavel and declared court in session. Their demeanor did not change all through the testimonies of the newly widowed Roberta Brown, who told of the threats that the Currys had made, and of the Brown children, who tearfully described what they had seen from the hayloft the day their father was killed.

The jury's deliberation took little more than an hour, and the spectators looked at each other knowingly as the six jurors filed back in. It was obvious to everyone that Reese would be convicted of murdering Darrell Brown and—given the reputation of Judge Thorne— subsequently sentenced to hang.

Facing the jury, Thorne asked the foreman, "Have you reached a verdict?"

The foreman stood and answered, "Yes, we have, Your Honor. We find the defendant not guilty. It is our unanimous opinion that Bud and Reese Curry were acting in self-defense when Darrell Brown went after them with the pitchfork."

The spectators collectively gasped, and then the courtroom erupted in shocked clamor—except Abner Curry and his bunch, who sat calmly. Long Shadow stood beside the defendant, who looked up and smiled smugly.

The judge, clearly furious, banged loudly on his desk with the gavel, demanding order. When silence settled over the room, Thorne twisted on his chair and glared at the jurors. "In my seventeen years as a judge I have never seen a jury act so imprudently! The witnesses who gave testimony left no doubt that the defendant and his deceased brother crept onto the Brown ranch with malicious intent, then threatened bodily harm to a woman and her small children. By finding in the defendant's favor you men have done your community a great injustice, and you ought to be ashamed of yourselves!"

A rumble of concurring voices filled the room.

The gavel pounded the desk and Thorne again demanded order. When peace was restored, the judge said grimly, "The law states that no one can be tried twice for the same crime. This duly authorized jury has acquitted the defendant, so my hands are tied." Looking at the killer, he announced, "Reese Curry, the jury has found you innocent of the murder of Darrell Brown. As much as it riles my sense of justice to the core, I must tell you that you are free to go."

The judge banged the gavel down hard and declared the court dismissed. Abner Curry's men whooped gleefully as the family members rushed to Reese, surrounding him. The six jurors slunk out of the courtroom, unable to look at any of their fellow citizens.

Shaking his head in disgust as he watched the jurors leave, Long Shadow turned back to look at the Currys and found Abner watching him with a gleam in his eyes. The rancher stepped closer to the lawman while his men were congratulating Reese and crowed, "Well, looks like the law was on our side, redskin."

"The only thing on your side was fear and intimidation," Long Shadow retorted. "You had your filthy hand in it, there's no doubt in my mind."

"You can't prove it," the stout-bodied man challenged.

The lawman stared unwaveringly at him for several seconds, then warned, "You and I are like two fast-moving trains, heading toward each other on the same track. One heck of a crash is due to come." With that, the tall Cheyenne pivoted and left.

Watching him go, Abner smirked. Then he walked over to Reese and threw an arm around his son's shoulders. "Come on. Let's go celebrate at the Broken Spur." Smiling at his hired hands, he added, "Drinks are on me, boys!"

As Reese Curry emerged from the town hall, an expression of victory on his face, the townspeople looked at him with contempt, angered that the killer they had figured was as good as hanged was walking away a free man. Disdainful of their opinion of him, the stocky young rancher led his entourage across the street to the saloon.

The Curry clan took a table by themselves while their ranch hands gathered at a table nearby. When a bottle was procured and shot glasses were full, Abner downed a glass in three gulps. After pouring another, he ran his nervous gaze over the faces of his sons and said quietly, "Boys, this thing ain't over yet."

"What do you mean, Pa?" Emmett asked.

"I saw that Indian givin' the jurymen the eye. He knows what we did as sure as I'm sittin' here—and as sure as I'm sittin' here he's gonna put pressure on 'em."

Jake guffawed. "Ain't gonna do him no good, Pa. We've got those jurors scared out of their wits. They know their families are in danger if they spill the beans. We reminded 'em about that Furman kid gettin' bashed on the head . . . and they all know Darrell Brown paid for standin' up to us. There ain't nothin' to worry about."

"Maybe not with the five who've got family," his father countered, "but Joe Cofield don't have family. Of all the jurors he was hardest to frighten in the first place. Since there's no family for him to worry about, he's liable to break under Long Shadow's pressuring."

"Seems to me that don't leave us much choice, Pa," Jake remarked. "Cofield'll have to be eliminated."

"It'll have to wait till night falls and we can catch him at his house," Abner said. "We sure can't make the attempt while he's behind his teller's window at the bank. In the meantime I'm gonna leave a couple of men to keep watch on the marshal and see if he questions the jurors like I suspect he will. Best thing for us to do is get on back home."

Twilight was settling over the Black Hills when Abner Curry's two men came back to inform him that Marshal Long Shadow had indeed visited all six jurymen during the afternoon. Cursing loudly, Abner then asked what time the lawman had seen Joseph Cofield.

"Just before five o'clock, boss," one of the men replied. "The marshal was in his house for about ten minutes."

Nodding, Abner told his sons, "Looks like we're okay so far, then. That was three hours ago, and if that stinkin' redskin had anything on us, he'd have been here by now. Apparently Cofield kept his mouth shut. But I ain't sure it'll stay that way. Reese and Jake, go into town and take care of Mr. Cofield. Just don't get yourselves caught."

"How about me goin' with 'em, Pa?" Emmett asked. "It's time I was gettin' in on some of the fun."

His older brothers exchanged knowing glances. Emmett was wasting his breath, for Abner Curry was not going to endanger his favorite son. Reese and Jake grinned at each other covertly as the elder Curry patted his youngest son's shoulder and said, "You just stay here with me, boy. Your brothers can handle it."

Thirty minutes later, under cover of darkness, Jake and Reese Curry ground-tied their horses behind Joseph Cofield's small house and crept up to a lighted kitchen window, peering in. The bank teller, who was in his early fifties, was seated in a chair, eating dinner.

"Okay," Reese whispered, "we'll take him by surprise. You have your gun ready while I kick the door in. We'll blow him to kingdom come, then ride as hard as we can."

"I'm ready," Jake whispered.

Stepping onto the back porch, the two stocky men lined up with the door. Reese pulled his revolver, cocked it, took a deep breath, and kicked the door violently. It gave way instantly, flying open. Joseph Cofield dropped his fork and gasped, his eyes bulging.

Reese was regaining his balance and bringing his gun to bear on the teller as Jake thundered in behind him. Suddenly a deep growl came from a corner of the room, and a huge black dog lunged at Reese, eyes wild and fangs bared.

Swinging his revolver from the man to the dog, Reese fired, and the dog yelped and went down in a heap, dead.

Cofield sprang out of his chair, terrified. Throwing his hands up, the teller begged, "Please! Don't shoot!"

"The marshal talked to you today, didn't he?" Jake demanded, aiming his gun at the middle-aged man.

"Yes, but I didn't tell him anything! Honest!"

"But you will when he squeezes good and hard. We can't take that chance."

Even as he spoke, Jake pulled the trigger. The gun roared, and Joseph Cofield went down with a bullet in his chest, sprawling beside his dog.

Voices suddenly sounded from the front yard as neighbors came on the run. Grabbing his brother's arm, Reese shouted, "Come on! Let's get outta here!"

Reese and Jake were barely out the back door when three armed men charged into the parlor. The brothers mounted their horses and galloped away in the darkness, but when they were a safe distance from town, thundering across the grassy hills, Jake shouted, "Reese! What if he ain't dead? We didn't take time to check!"

"He's dead, all right!" Reese shouted back. "You hit him square in the middle of the chest! A man can't live with a bullet in his heart! Don't worry, Joe Cofield ain't gonna tell the law nothin'. Dead men don't talk!"

# Chapter Nine

Shortly after nine o'clock, Marshal Long Shadow was reading in the parlor, and April Dawn had gone to make sure the children were sleeping when a series of rapid knocks sounded at the front door. Answering the summons, Long Shadow opened the door to find Joseph Cofield's next-door neighbor, Jasper Elkins, gasping for breath. His eyes wide, Elkins choked, "Marshal! Joe's been shot! Doc Tottingham's been sent for, but Joe knows he's dying. He wants to talk to you!"

Long Shadow darted down the hallway and called to his wife that he was going out, then ran as fast as he could to the teller's house, leaving the panting Elkins behind. Making his way through the streets, he soon crossed the small yard and pushed his way past a group of neighbors gathered on the porch. Rushing inside, he shouldered his way past several more men standing in the kitchen, surrounding Ronald Tottingham and the dying man. Cofield still lay on the kitchen floor where he had fallen, beside the body of his big black dog.

As Long Shadow broke through the circle he nodded at the kneeling Tottingham, then knelt himself on Cofield's other side. "He's hanging on, Marshal," the doctor said. "He's determined to talk to you."

Looking into the teller's face, the lawman saw the pallor of death already evident. The man's eyes were glassy, but they focused on him when he asked, "Joe, can you hear me? It's the marshal."

Cofield licked his dry lips and spoke haltingly in a weak voice. "Marshal, I . . . I . . ."

"Who did this to you, Joe?" Long Shadow pressed, glad for all the people in the room who would serve as witnesses to Joseph Cofield's last words.

Cofield tried to speak, but he was having difficulty. Although the marshal was certain that the assailant had been one of the Currys, he dared not put names in the mortally wounded man's mouth.

The dying man closed his eyes briefly, then tried again. Finally a feeble "Curry" came out.

"Curry?" repeated the marshal, looking around the room and making sure the other witnesses had heard. They all nodded gravely.

Cofield answered slowly, "Yes. Two . . . of them."

"Which two?" the Indian asked, bending lower.

Joseph Cofield's lips quivered. "Reese . . . J—" He coughed, spewing blood.

"Reese," Long Shadow echoed. "Go on," he urged. "Tell me the name of the other one."

Cofield coughed again, choked on the blood, gasped, and said, "Jake. It was . . . Jake."

"Reese and Jake Curry!" Long Shadow blurted. "They shot you?"

Cofield gurgled "Yes" and coughed once more, and his eyes closed. When his head lolled to the side, Dr. Tottingham checked his neck pulse, then looked at the marshal and shook his head.

Long Shadow stood up and eyed the neighbors in the room. "You all heard Joe's last words. Would you be willing to testify in court?"

The men agreed that they would.

"All right," the lawman declared, his face hardening.

"We're going to nail those scum this time. And I'm going to arrest them right now."

Standing, he strode outside. He was about to leave when one of the men caught up with him and said, "Long Shadow, it might be wise for you to take a posse with you. You just might run into a hornet's nest out there. Abner isn't going to be too congenial when you show up to arrest his sons."

"That's good advice, Marshal," called one of the other men standing on the porch. "I'll be glad to ride in the posse."

Rubbing his angular chin, Long Shadow nodded and said, "I appreciate the advice. All right. I'll take a posse along."

Immediately four more men volunteered. Long Shadow instructed them to see if they could find seven more townsmen who would ride with him to the Curry ranch. He would first go to Frank Denton's house to inform him of his teller's death, then go home and advise April Dawn of the situation. When that was done, he would return to the jail. "Tell everyone to meet me at my office as soon as you're ready," he directed.

An hour later, Long Shadow and the dozen men who had ridden across the moonlit prairie arrived at the Curry ranch, hauling up in the yard in a cloud of dust. They found Abner and Emmett sitting on the front porch, smoking cigarettes.

Instantly getting up from his chair, the rancher stepped to the edge of the porch and glared at Long Shadow, shouting, "What is it this time, lawman?"

While the others stayed in their saddles, Long Shadow dismounted and walked over to the house, answering the question with another question. "Where are Reese and Jake, Curry?"

"They went into town and haven't returned yet. Why?"

"Because Joseph Cofield was murdered."

Snorting with derision, Abner spat, "What's that got to do with my boys?"

"Your *boys* are the ones who killed him," the lawman retorted.

The rancher's face darkened with anger as he railed, "That's a lie! My sons wouldn't kill anyone! Even the jury knew that Reese was innocent—in spite of your empty accusations, Indian!"

Shaking his head slowly, Long Shadow rejoined, "This time you won't get away with it, Curry, because this time your victim lived long enough to name his killers . . . in front of witnesses." He paused, then continued, "I guarantee that Reese won't get acquitted this time. And if you try to tamper with the jury again, I'll send *you* to prison as well."

His bitterness apparent, Abner Curry snapped harshly, "I didn't tamper with no jury . . . and neither did my boys!"

"I have proof!" Long Shadow countered. "I visited Joe Cofield this afternoon, and he admitted that you and Jake threatened him before the trial. If he didn't vote for acquittal, he would suffer the consequences."

"Oh, yeah?" Abner growled. "Then why didn't you come after me and Jake?"

"Because I wanted to find another juror who would admit it as well. That would have given me a more substantial case against you. Unfortunately their fear kept them silent—but I know the truth."

"That's nonsense!" the rancher roared. "You couldn't find no one else 'cause we didn't do nothin'. Cofield must have had it in for us for some reason, so he lied about bein' threatened. And he lied again when he told

you Reese and Jake shot him down. My boys ain't
murderers!"

"Joe didn't lie!" the lawman exclaimed. "And quit
stalling! Where are Reese and Jake?"

"You deaf?" Abner snapped. "I've already told you
they ain't here. They ain't back from town yet. But
don't take my word for it. Search all you want."

"You're awfully eager to help," the marshal remarked
after a moment's hesitation. "Which means they're not
here. But I'm warning you: If your sons don't turn
themselves in and you hide them or help them escape,
you'll be obstructing justice—and that can get you at
least twenty years in prison."

Curry's face went livid with rage as he screamed in a
high-pitched voice, "You killed Bud! Took my oldest
son! My sons are all I have in the world! What more do
you want?"

Long Shadow answered levelly, "I want Jake and
Reese to pay for the murder of Joseph Cofield. That's
what I want—and that's what I'm going to get."

The malevolent rancher hissed, "If you're gonna search
the place, get it over with. If not, remove yourself and
your posse from my property."

The lawman walked toward his horse, calling over his
shoulder, "I'd be wasting my time. If they are here—
which is doubtful—there are too many places to hide in
the dark." Mounting, he settled in the saddle and said,
"Remember what I told you. If you harbor those fugi-
tive sons of yours, you'll look at the world through
prison bars for a long, long time."

Seething with hatred, Abner watched the posse ride
away. As soon as they were out of sight, he turned to
Emmett and urged, "Come on."

The Currys ran to the barn and threw open the door.
"Reese? Jake? You still in here?"

"Yeah, Pa," Reese answered from up in the hayloft. The two brothers climbed down the ladder and crossed the barn. "Good thing that you were shoutin' so loud, we realized what was goin' on. Or at least part of it—the part that warned us we'd better stay in here and keep out of sight."

"Yeah, that was my intention. I'm glad it worked. But you gotta get out of here tonight! That redskin'll be back in the mornin' for sure."

"What did he want, anyway?" Jake queried, smirking. "To throw more unproven accusations at us?"

Scowling, Abner responded, "They ain't unproven this time. Joe Cofield lived long enough to name you two as his killers. That stinkin' Indian and several other witnesses heard him tell everything. The lawman is wantin' to arrest you for murderin' Cofield, and let me tell you, he as good as had a rope in his hand. He ain't gonna rest till he sees you hang."

Jake popped a fist into his palm and swore. "I knew I should've shot Cofield again to make sure!"

"We didn't have time!" Reese countered. "Those neighbors were comin' on fast!"

"No sense arguin' about that now," Abner cut in. "You two gotta hit the saddle!"

"Where should we go, Pa?" Reese asked.

Rubbing his chin, Abner studied the floor. Finally he looked at Reese and replied, "You remember that abandoned cabin we stayed in for a couple days, when we first came through this country?"

"You mean the one over in Wyoming . . . near Devil's Tower?"

"Yeah. It's a good thirty miles from here, so that'd be a good place for you boys to hole up awhile till I eliminate Long Shadow."

The Curry brothers' shock was evident, and Jake was

the first to voice it. "Pa, what are you talkin' about? You've insisted all along that none of us should try to eliminate that scummy redskin, sayin' he'd kill us for sure! Now *you're* gonna try it?"

Slapping his palms against his thighs, the patriarch replied, "The way I see it, there ain't no choice. I just have to put my mind on *how* to kill him. It'll take some time to plan, but once he's dead, you boys can come back home."

Jake shook his head. "Pa, seems to me you ain't thinkin' too clear. What about all them other witnesses who heard Cofield name us as his killers? They'll just go to the next marshal of Cheyenne Crossing, and *he'll* arrest us."

Abner grinned. "The next marshal of Cheyenne Crossing will be owned by yours truly. He'll be in my hip pocket and do what I tell him. Money talks, and he'll make more money under the table from me in a month than the town pays him in a year. And as for them witnesses, threats have worked just fine before . . . no reason to think they won't work again. Don't worry, boys. Like I said, it might take some time, but things'll go our way."

The Currys went to the house and packed an ample supply of food into several gunnysacks for the two fugitives. During the process, Abner explained that as soon as Long Shadow was dead, he and Emmett would ride to the cabin and let Reese and Jake know.

Jake asked, "Pa, what if there's somebody stayin' in that old cabin?"

"Kill him," came the flat reply. "I want you boys there so I'll know where to find you. Understand?"

"Yes, sir," Jake assured him.

Reese was opening and closing cupboard doors furiously, mumbling to himself.

"What you lookin' for?" his father asked.

"Whiskey, Pa! I don't want to hole up in that cabin without whiskey!"

"Well, if you don't see any, we must be out. You'll have to live without it."

Reese swore and cinched his gunnysack closed.

As the two older sons tied the sacks to their saddle pommels and mounted their horses at the front porch, Jake said, "Pa, you be careful about killin' that redskin. Don't take no chances."

"I won't, son," the rancher promised.

"Maybe you oughta hire some professional killer, Pa," Reese ventured. "I sure don't want nothin' to happen to you."

"I'll give it some thought," the elder Curry said with a nod. "Now, you boys get goin'."

Emmett told his brothers good-bye, and they saluted him and galloped away, heading northwest toward the Wyoming border. Ten minutes later, when the moonlit buildings of Cheyenne Crossing came into view, Reese called above the rumble of the hooves, "Let's swing into town and get some whiskey."

"It's past midnight! There's no saloon open at this time of night!"

"I know, but I figure I can break into the Pine Tree and steal a few bottles. I ain't holin' up in that cabin without whiskey!"

The brothers hauled up under a stand of pine trees on the west side of town. Jake remained in his saddle when Reese dismounted and, looking down at him, argued, "This is too risky, Reese. It ain't worth takin' chances like this."

"Don't fret, Jake," his younger brother countered as he walked away. "I'll be back in a few minutes."

Keeping to the shadows, Reese stalked cautiously

along a side street until he reached Main Street. The saloon was a block away, and he slowly and carefully inched his way down the street, constantly looking in both directions until he arrived at his destination.

Cheyenne Crossing had streetlamps seventy feet apart, and as he hugged the front of the saloon, Reese spotted the marshal a block away. Long Shadow was making his rounds, moving slowly as he checked store doors to see if they were locked. He was heading in Reese's direction, but Reese figured if he broke a window at the back of the Pine Tree, the marshal would never hear it.

Dashing to the rear of the saloon, he used the butt of his gun to break a pane, unlocked the window, and climbed in. Three minutes later, cradling four whiskey bottles, he had one leg out the window and was about to drag the other one over the sill when two of the bottles slipped from his fingers. They crashed to the ground, sending a shattering sound echoing off the surrounding buildings.

Swearing under his breath, Reese planted both feet on the ground and was about to run when from behind him a voice said loudly, "Figuring on going somewhere, Reese?"

The young rancher gasped, dropped the other bottles, and clawed for his gun. He never cleared leather. The butt of Long Shadow's revolver chopped him solidly on the back of his head, and he went down, unconscious.

Jake Curry waited restlessly at the edge of town, wondering what was keeping his brother. Nearly an hour had passed since Reese had gone to burglarize the Pine Tree Saloon—an operation that should have taken no more than twenty minutes. After several more minutes had passed he was certain that something had gone wrong, so he picked up the reins of Reese's horse and headed back to the ranch.

Awakening Abner Curry, Jake told him what had occurred. "The only thing I could figure, Pa," he concluded, "is that Reese got caught. I was afraid to stay any longer for fear I might be next."

"You did the right thing, son," Abner told him. "And just in case Long Shadow decides to come back out here tonight, you'd better hide. Probably the best place is the storage cellar under the bunkhouse. The whole aisle is covered with a runner, so no one will even know the trapdoor's there. The boys won't say nothin'; they've proved their loyalty by now. I'll send a couple of 'em into town first thing in the mornin' to nose around and see if they can learn somethin' about Reese."

Returning from town the next morning on foam-flecked horses, Curry's riders galloped up to the front porch and reported that Reese had indeed been caught and was in jail. Abner sent them to the corral, then stormed into the house with Emmett following. Entering the den, he screamed profanities, kicked chairs, and threw books across the room.

He had just calmed down slightly when Emmett looked out the den window and told him Long Shadow was riding into the yard with his twelve-man posse. Swearing again, Abner said he had better go meet the marshal at the porch, otherwise Long Shadow would surely force his way into the house.

The lawman was dismounting as the rancher wrenched open the door. Abner halted in the middle of the porch and waited for the marshal to speak.

Long Shadow walked across the yard and stood at the bottom of the porch steps. Shoving back his white

Stetson, he remarked, "I was told that a couple of your men were in town this morning, so you obviously know that I've got Reese in jail. Where's Jake?"

"I have no idea," Curry lied, making no attempt to mask his hatred for the Cheyenne.

"Of course not," the marshal retorted sardonically. "Well, we're going to search the place anyway."

The marshal assigned the possemen to look through the house and all the outbuildings, while he himself searched the bunkhouse. Worry scratched at Abner Curry's mind as he followed Long Shadow across the yard. Several ranch hands were in the bunkhouse as the marshal entered, got down on his knees and looked under every bed, investigated the closets, and paced slowly down the long aisle between the beds.

Abner and Emmett waited near the door, deliberately not looking at the end of the aisle, where the trapdoor to the cellar was located. After a few moments the lawman strode back to the front of the bunkhouse and told the rancher, "Sooner or later I'll catch Jake. Oh, by the way, Judge Thorne is on his way from Deadwood. He'll be in town tomorrow to hold Reese's trial. And just in case you have the notion to bring in a bunch of your hired hands and attempt to break Reese out of jail, you should know that the entire posse will be on guard until he hangs."

The courtroom was again packed the next day when Judge Emery Thorne presided over Reese Curry's second murder trial. Marshal Long Shadow gave testimony of Joseph Cofield's last words, which had named Reese and Jake Curry as his killers, and the four witnesses following him to the stand corroborated the lawman's deposition.

Though fearful of Abner Curry, the jurymen delivered a unanimous guilty verdict—anything less would have brought the town down on their heads—and a trembling Reese Curry was ushered to the judge's desk by Long Shadow.

Judge Thorne fixed the guilty man with cold eyes and said, "Reese Curry, you have been found guilty of murdering Joseph Cofield. You are hereby sentenced to hang by your neck until dead." Taking a moment to look at a small desk calendar, Thorne proceeded, "Your crime was cold-blooded and heinous. I want you to have time to think about it . . . and to contemplate your execution. Therefore you will be hanged four days hence, on May 18. I would suggest that in the course of your time left on earth you repent—before the sudden stop at the end of the rope ushers you into the presence of your Maker."

Thorne waited until Long Shadow and the posse had escorted Reese Curry out of the building and back to the jail before dismissing the court. Abner and his men filed out slowly, then went immediately to the saloon. Huddled around a table together, the ranch hands asked Curry what he was going to do.

Downing a shot of whiskey, the grim-faced man responded, "I don't know yet. But you can bet your best pair of boots I ain't gonna let my boy hang. I'm sure relieved the judge put the hangin' off for a few days. Gives me more time to work out a plan."

Emmett looked scared. "Pa, you've got to get Reese out of this! I don't want to lose another brother!"

Looking affectionately at his youngest son, the rancher said, "Neither do I, boy. Don't you worry none. I'll come up with somethin' in time to get Reese out of that redskin's hands. You ain't gonna lose another brother."

Leaving the saloon, Abner and his bunch made their way to where they had left their horses. The rancher was about to untie his mount from the hitch rail when, looking over the horse's back, he saw April Dawn and her two children entering a store.

They passed from view, and Abner grinned wickedly. Stepping into the stirrup and swinging into the saddle, he chuckled and said to Emmett and the others, "I just came up with the solution to our problem, boys. Reese ain't gonna hang. I guarantee it."

# Chapter Ten

Long Shadow and his family finished eating supper, and April Dawn poured out coffee for herself and her husband. Picking up his cup, the lawman drank the steaming liquid, slurping loudly, and the children laughed with unbridled delight at his noisy display.

Shaking her head in wry disbelief, April Dawn mockingly scolded her husband. "You are setting quite an example for your son and daughter, Long Shadow! Do you want them to think it is acceptable to make that awful noise when they drink?"

The marshal grinned. "You shouldn't scold me. After all, your coffee is so delicious, it must be slurped to show how good it is!"

Rolling her eyes, April Dawn shook her head again. "What am I to do with such a man?"

"Love him in spite of his slurping," came the marshal's answer.

She laughed. "I will do that, my husband! However, I will never love the slurping!"

After a while their conversation turned to the upcoming hanging, and the children listened intently to their parents' discussion.

"Papa," Little Sun interjected, "can I go to the hanging?"

"No. Neither of you will go," their father said flatly.

"You will undoubtedly see enough violence in your lives. Watching a man die on the gallows is too much for your young eyes."

While April Dawn poured more coffee, she remarked to her husband, "Abner Curry is a very crafty man. I feel sure he will make some kind of attempt to free Reese before the hanging."

The handsome Cheyenne disagreed. "There is no way he can do that, my sweet. I have the jail well fortified with a virtual army of men. This time Mr. Reese Curry is going to hang. Sooner or later, I'll catch Jake as well, and the same noose that brings justice to his brother will administer justice to him."

"But the Currys have more ranch hands than you have possemen," the black-haired beauty argued as she poured cream into her cup. "Could that not give them enough advantage to break Reese out?"

Setting his cup down, Long Shadow answered, "As a matter of fact, I've recruited a lot more men. Abner Curry will find it impossible to handle my army. His son is going to hang on Friday, and if he's stupid enough to try anything, Abner Curry will end up behind bars . . . or dead."

When April Dawn and her children had finished lunch the following day, she smiled at them and asked if they had had enough to eat.

"Your cooking is so good," Little Sun responded, "I could never get enough of it."

April Dawn laughed and tousled her son's thick, dark hair. "My, aren't you the charmer? I declare, you are getting more like your father every day!"

Her black eyes wide, the little girl looked up at her mother and asked, "Am I getting more like *you* every day, Mama?"

"No, you aren't!" her big brother said, giggling. "Mama is beautiful!"

Star Light stuck her tongue out at her brother as April Dawn said in mock exasperation, "Okay, you two. It is a beautiful day. Go outside and play."

"I wish Papa were here to play with us," Little Sun mused.

Smiling, April Dawn told him, "I'm sure your papa wishes the same thing. Unfortunately, he was too busy at the office to even come home for lunch, much less have time to play with you."

Sighing, the two children ran out the back door, while their mother occupied herself with cleaning up the kitchen. As the afternoon wore on, April Dawn was busy doing household chores, periodically glancing out an open window and smiling as a particularly happy peal of laughter or squeal of delight came from the children as they played around the house and barn.

Some two hours had passed when Star Light ran across the back porch and bolted through the kitchen door, panting. "Can I have a drink of water, Mama?" she asked.

Getting up from the kitchen table, where she had been sitting and shelling peas, April Dawn replied, "Of course." She walked to the sink and worked the pump handle. Soon a stream of water flowed, and the Cheyenne woman held a porcelain cup to the flow.

Given the cup, Star Light drank rapidly, saying between gulps, "We're playing . . . hide and seek. Little Sun thought . . . he had fooled me when he . . . hid under the porch." She smiled triumphantly. "But I found him!"

Setting down the empty cup, the child dashed out of the house, letting the screen door slam behind her.

Star Light bounded off the porch and looked toward

the gate of the small corral where she had last seen her brother. He was not there. She rotated in a complete circle, scanning the backyard, but there was no sign of Little Sun. Figuring he had gone to the front yard, she ran there and looked under the front porch, thinking Little Sun had decided to hide in the same spot where he had hidden earlier. But he was not there, either.

Annoyed, she impatiently cupped her hands to her mouth and called, "Little Sun! Where are you? It's no fair hiding when I'm in the house!"

She waited for a response. When it did not come, she darted once again to the backyard. After checking the outhouse and finding it empty, she went to the barn. She slipped in through the partly open door and surveyed the dim interior. "Little Sun? Are you in here?" she called. "If you are, you're in trouble! We're not supposed to play in here without Mama and Papa!" She waited a few moments, then took a tentative step farther in. Peering into the corners, she called again, "Little Sun, come out!" But there was no response.

She stepped back outside, and the bright sun momentarily blinded her. Shading her eyes, her back to the barn door, she looked around the yard; her brother was nowhere to be seen. She continued calling his name, but she received no answer. Star Light began having dark thoughts about her brother, and pouting, she walked back to the house, angrily kicking pebbles that stood in her path.

Sitting at the table, mending a tear in one of her aprons, April Dawn looked up when she heard her daughter indignantly stomp into the house. When she saw the expression on Star Light's face, she knew immediately that something was wrong. "Goodness!" she exclaimed. "Did you and your brother have an argument?"

"He's playing a trick on me, Mama. When I came in before to get my drink of water, he hid someplace, and now I can't find him. I called to him over and over, but he won't come out. Will you holler at him and make him come out and play with me?"

Sighing, April Dawn went outside and called to her son from the back porch, telling him to play fair with his sister. When there was no response, she walked the yard, calling to him. The teenage boy who lived next door hopped off his porch and came toward April Dawn, asking what was wrong. She explained about Little Sun's disappearance, and the youth offered to help look for the boy.

He and April Dawn scouted the neighborhood for the next thirty minutes, looking in yards and inquiring if people had seen Little Sun. When he was nowhere to be found, April Dawn grew frightened and asked the teenager to go to the marshal's office and fetch Long Shadow.

Learning of Little Sun's disappearance, Long Shadow hurried home to find his wife frantic. The lawman listened to the account of the boy's disappearance and became concerned, for it was not like his son to wander off without seeking permission. Hoping it was merely a matter of the boy being thoughtless, Long Shadow nonetheless enlisted several of his neighbors to help them locate Little Sun.

Long Shadow kept his wife and daughter with him for the rest of the afternoon as they walked the dusty streets and alleys, searching diligently—but to no avail. Darkness was descending over Cheyenne Crossing when all the searchers met back at the marshal's office. No one had seen any sign of Little Sun. Thanking them for their help, Long Shadow told them he would appreciate their assistance again in the morning to continue the search. This time they would leave the town's boundaries and look on the prairie and through the hills.

Picking up his exhausted daughter and cradling her in one arm, Long Shadow put his other arm around his wife and said, "Come, darling. Let's go home."

As the disheartened family walked slowly through town, April Dawn suddenly burst into tears. Clinging to her husband, she cried, "Oh, Long Shadow! I feel it in my bones that something dreadful has happened to Little Sun!"

Affected by her mother's worry, Star Light also began to weep, and Long Shadow tried to calm them by saying everything would turn out all right. Maybe the boy had seen one of the ranchers' sons on the street and decided to take a ride with him somewhere.

Reaching their house, they stepped up on the front porch and saw a sheet of paper tacked to the door. Long Shadow removed the note and tried to read it, but it was too dark.

Groping his way into the gloom of the parlor, he found the lamp on the small side table and lit the wick. As the room filled with light, he held the sheet of paper so that his wife could read it as well:

Marshal—

I have your son in a hidden place several miles from town. Free Reese and tell him I am at the cabin. He'll know where I am. Do not follow him! You pushed me into this. If Reese isn't at the cabin by noon tomorrow, your son dies. If you follow Reese, your son dies. And if you think you can get the information any other way, think again. My other sons are coming with me, and none of my men knows where the cabin is. Do as I say and you'll get the kid back alive in due time.

Abner Curry

Feeling terror burning through her heart like acid, April Dawn gripped her husband's muscular arms and begged, "You've got to let Reese go! If you don't, that heartless animal will carry out his threat!"

Star Light yanked on the sleeve of her mother's dress, asking what the note said. April Dawn looked down at her and in a pained voice explained that a bad man had kidnapped Little Sun. Not understanding the full implication of what her mother had just told her, the child watched April Dawn carefully, observing her reactions.

April Dawn turned her attention back to Long Shadow, whose eyes seemed to be staring off into another world. Shaking him, she demanded, "You will let him go, won't you?"

Her husband's eyes were colder than she had ever seen them, and his body was so stiff it seemed as though he might snap in two. Looking down at April Dawn, his eyes softened and he replied, "I will rescue our boy. And I will make Abner Curry wish he had never been born."

"Listen to me!" the frantic mother shrieked. "You must turn Reese loose! You read what his father said! If Reese does not arrive by noon tomorrow, our son will be killed!"

Star Light began sobbing, and the tall Indian reached down and picked her up, holding her close. The girl lay her head on his shoulder and hugged his neck tightly, whimpering, "Papa, what will the bad man do to Little Sun?"

"Nothing, honey," he told her softly. "Papa will rescue your brother."

Extending his free hand, Long Shadow reached through April Dawn's long, black hair and took hold of the back of her neck. Pressing gently but firmly, he said, "You must understand, darling. I cannot let Reese Curry out of jail. This badge I wear won't let me. The man is a murderer, tried and convicted in a court of law. His death sentence must be carried out."

Reaching up and squeezing his wrist, the beautiful woman argued fiercely, "Is our son not more important than your badge or the law? Please! Go and release Reese right now so he can go to his father!"

His face showing the burden he was under, Long Shadow countered, "If instead of Little Sun it was someone else's little boy in danger, would you think a murderer should be set free?"

April Dawn bit her lip and shook her head. "No, Long Shadow, I would not," she admitted. "I am sorry I argued with you."

"You have nothing to be sorry for," he murmured. "It's only natural that you feel as you do. If I didn't wear a badge, I would feel no differently. However, I must uphold the law. But I give you my solemn vow that I will rescue our son."

"But how? Can you find this cabin by noon tomorrow?"

"We must pray to the Great Spirit, asking for help."

Ten minutes later, Long Shadow stormed into the cellblock, carrying Abner Curry's note and shouting Reese Curry's name. The killer rose from his bunk and walked to the bars, and when he did, the angry lawman shook the paper in his face and ordered, "Read this!"

Reese took the paper, angled it toward the lantern burning on the outside wall, and slowly read. A malicious grin spread over his face, and when he handed the paper back to the marshal, he sneered, "Well, whaddya know? So Pa's got your kid? I knew he'd do somethin' to save my neck!"

Fresh fury roiled through the Cheyenne. "Tell me where the cabin is!" he roared.

Smirking, Reese replied, "I'd be a fool to tell you. And let me make this real clear, redskin: When my pa says he'll kill your kid if I ain't at the cabin by noon tomorrow, he means it! He also ain't kiddin' when he says he'll kill the kid if you follow me. Best thing for you to do is unlock the door and let me go . . . right now."

Bending down so as to stare directly into Reese's eyes, the marshal proclaimed, "You are not getting out! You are going to hang!"

The killer looked at him incredulously. "Hangin' me means so much to you that you'll let your kid die? Well, seems to me you better think about what's really important to you." Laughing, Reese added, "I'm sure after you've thought hard for a couple of hours, you'll change your mind. You ain't gonna let your kid die over the likes of me."

Anger surged through the Indian. Reaching through the bars, he grabbed the stocky man's shirt with both hands and yanked him hard, pressing the killer's face between the bars.

Holding him there, the marshal growled, "You tell me where the cabin is, or I'll come in there and beat it out of you!"

Reese merely laughed again. "You ain't gonna do that! You're a lawman. Lawmen can't go into a prisoner's cell and beat him up!"

Long Shadow knew the killer was right. Even a judge as tough as Emery Thorne would frown on a lawman who abused his office and beat a prisoner to a pulp. Disgusted, the Indian released him and trudged home.

April Dawn was waiting up for him, and her countenance fell when Long Shadow told her that he had been unable to learn anything. "What will you do now?" she asked wearily, holding on to her husband for strength.

"I'm not sure yet. I've been asking the Great Spirit for help, and perhaps if I concentrate hard enough, I will find the answer I need." Looking into her exhausted face, he told her tenderly, "You should go to bed, my darling."

"I cannot sleep with my son in the hands of that hellish beast," she countered.

Hugging her tightly, he breathed, "I know. But if you lie down, your body will be able to rest." He held her from him. "Go on. Star Light will need your strength tomorrow, so you must replenish it as best you can."

Long Shadow paced the floor almost all night, trying to come up with an idea that would lead to the rescue of his son. Dawn was breaking when he recalled Reese's words that a lawman could not beat information out of a prisoner. Suddenly he had his answer.

He whirled around to head for the bedroom and found April Dawn standing at the parlor door. Her hair was tousled and her dark eyes were bleary. "I know what I am going to do," he told her triumphantly.

Her face perked up. "What is that, Long Shadow?"

"When Reese kissed you and slapped Little Sun, I gave him a beating—not as marshal of this town but as a private citizen. Well, I will take another brief leave of absence—and I will beat him until he tells me where to find the cabin. It shouldn't take long."

"But a private citizen cannot unlock a cell door and enter a cell," she pointed out.

Smiling, he replied, "I'll take Barry Hawkins with me. As soon as I unlock the door as the marshal, I'll enter the cell and toss Barry the badge, taking my leave nance fell when Long Shadow told her that he had been unable to learn anything. "What will you do now?" she asked wearily, holding on to her husband for strength.

After kissing April Dawn firmly, Long Shadow rode to Barry Hawkins's house and found him eating breakfast. Hurriedly, Long Shadow explained his plan, and the two men dashed to the marshal's office.

Walking past the armed guards, they entered the cellblock together and stood before the bars. Reese sat up on his bunk and asked, "Decide to let me go, Marshal?"

"Absolutely not," Long Shadow retorted. "I *have* decided to do what I did the day you put your filthy mouth on my wife. I'm taking a leave of absence as town marshal, and as a private citizen whose son's life is in danger, I'm going to have a little talk with the scum who knows where my son is being held. Another good beating should get me the information."

Reese's body went rigid, and his face filled with fear. "Now, wait a minute, Marshal!" he gasped, his hand fingering the scars on his face. "This ain't right! I'll tell the judge! He'll—"

"He'll pat me on the back!" Long Shadow cut in roughly. "Have you forgotten the loathing he has for you?" As he spoke the tall lawman placed the key in thecell door.

"No! Wait a minute!" Reese yelled. "I'll tell you where the cabin is!"

Holding his hand on the inserted key, Long Shadow snapped, "Make it fast."

Asking for a piece of paper and a pencil, the killer drew the marshal a map and thrust it into his hand through the bars, saying, "It . . . it's a good two-hour ride, if you go at it hard. But don't let Pa know it was me who told you!"

"He'll probably figure it out without my help," Long Shadow remarked dryly. Turning to the part-time deputy, he said, "Barry, stay close to this animal and keep a sharp eye on him until I return."

# Chapter Eleven

April Dawn could bear the wait no longer. Immediately after Star Light had eaten breakfast, the harried woman took her daughter over to the Tottinghams' house. She knocked on the door, and her summons was quickly answered by Sally Tottingham.

The young physician immediately gave her friend a comforting hug. Stepping back, she offered, "Come in, you two," and after quickly assessing April Dawn's distraught face, Sally squatted down to Star Light's level. "Why don't you run into the kitchen, honey?" she suggested to the little girl. "I bet Uncle Ron can find you a sweet roll, if you tell him you'd like one."

"Okay," the child responded, and raced to find Ronald Tottingham.

Sally then led her friend into the parlor and sat down beside her on the couch. "I can tell by the look on your face that you have not yet found Little Sun."

Shaking her head and fighting back her tears, April Dawn softly replied, "No. You do know that Little Sun was kidnapped?"

The blonde sighed, nodding. "Yes. I'm sure the entire town knows by now. I still can't believe that Abner Curry has gone to such despicable and cruel lengths. To threaten a child with death if his killer son isn't released . . . why, it's positively inhuman."

137

April Dawn looked down at her lap, and the tears that she had struggled to contain spilled onto her cheeks. "Oh, Sally, it has been so hard for me to maintain my composure in front of Star Light. I did not want to frighten her even more than she already is, but now that the entire night has passed without my son, I cannot keep pretending any longer." Putting her head in her hands, she sobbed quietly for a few minutes, while Sally cradled her in her arms, rocking her softly as she would a child.

Finally composing herself, the Cheyenne woman explained, "Long Shadow went to the office soon after dawn, determined to get the location of the cabin out of Reese Curry—beating it out of him, if necessary. But I cannot wait any longer to find out if he was successful. Would it be possible for me to leave Star Light with you while I go to the office? I would rather not have to have her with me when I go there . . . just in case the news is bad."

"Of course I'll watch her!" Sally exclaimed. "Don't worry. Take all the time you need. And if Long Shadow has left and you want to stay there and wait for him, I'll understand." She looked at the watch pinned to the front of her crisp white blouse, checking the time. "Tell you what," she continued. "If you haven't returned by the time Ron has to open the clinic, I'll stay here with Star Light."

"But that would not be right," April Dawn protested.

Standing, still holding her friend's hand, Sally insisted, "Nonsense! We frequently have slow days—and perhaps this will be one of them. If Ron needs my help, he can send someone to get me, and I'll simply take Star Light back with me. The last thing I want you to do is worry unnecessarily. You have enough on your mind. Now, go on. Go see what Long Shadow has found out."

Smiling through her tears, April Dawn thanked Sally for her help. She dried her eyes and hurried into the kitchen to explain to her daughter that she would be staying with Aunt Sally for a short while, then ran to her husband's office. As she passed a side street she saw a group of small boys playing, and her heart ached even more for Little Sun. Would the Great Spirit answer her prayer and return her son alive and unharmed?

Reaching the marshal's office, April Dawn passed through a phalanx of armed men, murmuring greetings to each of them. "Good morning, Mr. Halberry," she said to the man who stood closest to the office door. "Is my husband still here?"

"No, ma'am. He rode out about an hour ago, maybe a little more. Sure am sorry about your boy, but your husband is a resourceful man. I'm sure this whole thing will turn out all right."

Again the Indian woman had to fight to maintain her composure. Strain showed in her eyes, and deep lines were etched in her brow. "Do you know if Long Shadow learned the location of the cabin from Reese Curry?"

Scratching his head, Halberry replied, "Well, I'm not really sure, ma'am. Our shift came on duty after your husband and Barry Hawkins were already inside. All I can tell you is that the marshal came out of the office like a bullet out of a barrel, leapt on his horse, and took off like the wind."

April Dawn nodded absently as she stepped inside. Hawkins was not in the office, which undoubtedly meant he was in the cellblock, so she hurried across the room and opened the door. The gunsmith was sitting in a chair facing the killer's cell, and he turned at the sound of the opening door, his gun held at the ready.

"Good morning, Barry," she called. "May I talk with you a moment?"

"Sure," Hawkins replied, a sympathetic expression on his face. Casting a quick glance at the prisoner, who sat on his bunk, he said, "We can talk in the office."

The Cheyenne woman continued into the cellblock. "No need," she responded. "I just want to know if my husband learned the location of the cabin where Little Sun is being held."

Chuckling, Hawkins told her, "He sure did. Long Shadow scared Reese enough that he drew him a map and everything. He's been gone for better than an hour."

April Dawn's hand went to her mouth and tears of relief welled up in her eyes. "Oh, I'm so glad! That's wonderful news, Barry!"

"Yep. Nothing to worry about now," Hawkins assured her. "The marshal will get the advantage over the Currys real quick—you know how he operates—and Little Sun will be back in his own bed tonight."

The burly prisoner's sudden, harsh laugh echoed off the cellblock walls.

Hawkins's head whipped around. "What's so funny, Curry?"

Snorting, Reese replied, "Nothin' much . . . just that I gave that stupid lawman the wrong directions. By the time he figures out that I sent him on a wild goose chase, he'll be miles in the opposite direction"—he looked at April Dawn, smirking—"and it'll be too late to save your brat! There sure ain't no way Long Shadow can engineer a rescue by noon when he'll still be tryin' to find his way back to where he started!"

Reese laughed gleefully. Then his laughter died, and he snarled, "Pa'll kill Little Sun, all right—and he'll come up with *another* way to free me before Friday!"

April Dawn's blood turned cold. Something had to be

done. "How far is that cabin from here, Reese?" she demanded.

"Why do you want to know that?" Hawkins asked.

Ignoring the deputy, she pressed the killer, "Is there still time to get to the cabin by noon?"

"Well, now, that's hard to say, honey," Reese drawled, grinning. "It's quite a ways from here, and there's lots of forest to pass through. Ain't like ridin' on open prairie. The goin' is mighty slow sometimes. But if you'll talk this here deputy into lettin' me out, I'll ride straight for the cabin and try to get there in time to save your son's life. Deal?"

The Cheyenne woman turned and looked sharply at Hawkins.

The deputy's face stiffened. "No, ma'am!" he blurted, knowing what she was thinking. "I'm not letting him loose! Your husband would have my hide! Besides, you can't believe a thing these Currys say. I'm not so sure Abner would let Little Sun live, even if he got Reese back."

"I can handle a gun as well as any man, Barry," the desperate mother told him. "Let's you and me handcuff this beast and make him take us to the cabin. The only chance I have to save my son is to strike a bargain with Abner. My son for his."

"No!" Hawkins blared, shaking his head vigorously. "Your husband told me in no uncertain terms to stay right here and keep an eye on Reese. I intend to do just that!"

Enraged, April Dawn made a fast move and snatched Hawkins's gun from his holster. Leaping out of his reach, she cocked the hammer and pointed the weapon straight at the prisoner. The beefy man's face blanched.

Hawkins took a step toward her, but April Dawn commanded, "Stop! One more step, and I'll kill Reese!"

The gunsmith froze in his tracks.

His eyes riveted on the ominous barrel centered on his chest, Reese blurted, "Hawkins, you gotta do somethin'!"

"Yes, you do!" April Dawn snapped. "Take those keys off your belt and open the cell."

"April Dawn, listen to me," the gunsmith said, trying to be calm. "That gun you're holding is one that I worked on. It has an extra-sensitive hair trigger, which means the very slightest movement will drop the hammer. And the cartridges are packed with a new, high-powered gunpowder. That .45 slug fired at close range will blow a hole in a man as big as a cabbage."

"Good!" she declared, showing her teeth in fury. "Then do what I tell you, Barry, before I get nervous and kill this sorry excuse for a human being! Now, unlock that cell and handcuff him, then give me the key!"

Reluctantly, Hawkins obeyed. After he had finished handcuffing Reese, he carefully dropped the key in her skirt pocket.

"All right," April Dawn breathed. "Now, the three of us are going to walk to the office. You go first, Barry, and I'll follow this slime. One false move, Reese, and you're gone. My son's life is at stake, so if I have any reason to believe you're going to try something, I will blow a hole through your back!"

Hawkins led the way, and when they had reached the office, the Indian woman ordered, "Now, Barry, go out ahead of us, and tell those guards to bring up two saddled horses. No delays. When they're ready, let me know, and Reese and I will come out. This gun will be pointed at him every moment, even while I am mounting, so if anybody tries to stop me, I will shoot. Go on, Barry. Make it fast."

While the gunsmith was outside explaining the situation to the armed men, and horses were being brought up, the prisoner, his face beading with sweat, swallowed hard and asked, "You ain't gonna ride with that gun pointed at me, are you? I mean, the slightest bump and—"

"The gun stays cocked and aimed at you all the way, mister!" April Dawn bellowed with finality.

Barry Hawkins returned, telling April Dawn the horses were ready and assuring her the guards would not interfere. Nodding, she directed Reese outside, finding a crowd of spectators had gathered. April Dawn stayed close while the prisoner hoisted himself into the saddle, and then she tore a long strip of fabric from the hem of her red calico dress. Looking intently at the guards and the people of Cheyenne Crossing, she told them loudly, "All of you, listen to me! My son's life is in danger. If I do not get Reese to his father's hideout by noon, Abner will kill my son. If anyone makes a move in my direction, I will take it as a threat to stop me, and I swear I will kill Reese!" Holding up the red fabric, she added, "Tell Long Shadow that I will leave a trail for him to follow."

A wide circle was made for April Dawn as she carefully mounted the horse provided for her. Guiding it up behind Reese Curry, who sat gripping the reins with his shackled hands, she stated vehemently, "Let me inform you that I am the daughter of the late Chief Black Thunder, a fierce warrior. You would no doubt call him a savage. Well, his blood runs through my veins, and this savage will be at your back all the way. Try any tricks or lead me in the wrong direction, and I'll kill you."

"I understand," the frightened killer mumbled.

"Good. Time is moving swiftly. We had better do the same."

Believing the Cheyenne woman meant business, the townsmen only watched as the duo rode out, April Dawn holding the hair-trigger revolver pointed directly at Reese's back.

Abner Curry's cabin hideout was nestled in the trees at the edge of a dense forest on a rock-studded hillside. From its shadowed position it overlooked a broad meadow patched with clumps of tall brush and trees, with a small creek angling its way across the meadow like a twisted silver ribbon. Beyond the western edge of the meadow lay more forest, and rising some twelve hundred feet above the trees, looming like a monument erected by giants, was Devil's Tower.

The three-room log cabin had a peaked roof and a front porch running the length of the house. The cabin's large main room served as both kitchen and parlor, and the other two rooms were for sleeping.

The occupants of the cabin were all in the main room. Little Sun was forced to sit on the floor, while Abner, Jake, and Emmett Curry ringed their chairs around a rustic old table. Abner, his meaty arms folded across his chest, rocked his chair back on its hind legs. He had a cigarette dangling from the corner of his mouth, and he watched the Indian boy through the tendrils of smoke curling toward the beamed ceiling.

Jake, who always wore a large hunting knife in addition to his revolver, was sharpening the knife on a small flat rock, and the sound of metal rubbing stone filled the room.

Emmett rolled up the cuffs of his plaid shirt, then twirled his black Stetson on his finger, looking thoughtful. Finally he remarked, "Pa, we're ruined in these parts. We'll have to hightail it once we have Reese back with us."

Abner let the chair come down onto all four legs, sighed, and took the cigarette from his mouth. Flicking ashes on the floor, he responded, "Yeah, I'm afraid you're right about that, son. Even if we killed that scaly Indian lawman, we still couldn't stay around here. I was thinkin' that we'd be able to continue on the way we was, but the truth is the people'd hound us to death. I sure hate havin' to give up the ranch we so cleverly stole, but I guess there ain't no choice."

Lifting his thick body off the chair, the rancher stuck the cigarette back in his mouth and said, "Well, we can always steal another ranch somewhere. The main thing is I have you boys with me. Without my sons, life wouldn't be worth livin'." Tears misted his eyes as he added, "I miss Bud somethin' fierce."

For several minutes there was only the sound of the knife rubbing the rock.

Blowing a lungful of smoke toward the ceiling, Abner finally stood and walked over to Little Sun, telling him raggedly, "But I'll be gettin' my boy Reese back. Your old man ain't about to hang him, kid. I've seen how he feels about you. You mean as much to him as my sons mean to me. If the tables were turned, I'd sure let a prisoner outta jail to spare my boy."

The boy's dark eyes glared up at Abner Curry with silent hatred.

Breaking into a hoarse laugh, Abner added, "Only thing is . . . even when Reese walks through that door, I ain't lettin' you go. Once I've got my son back, you're dead. An eye for an eye is my philosophy. Your old man killed a son of mine. Now I'll kill one of his. Ain't my fault you're the only son he has."

Feeling his heart pounding, Little Sun was completely terrified. His breath came in short gasps, and he felt as though he were not getting enough air into his lungs.

The elder Curry laughed again. "Scared, huh, kid? Well, you can blame your old man. It's his fault you're in this mess."

Abner turned and went back to his chair, and a few moments later the men were so intensely caught up in their conversation that they seemed to forget the boy was there. As he thought of the rancher's words Little Sun realized that if he was going to survive, he would have to find a way to escape, and his gaze drifted to the open doorway. Maybe if he could get a good enough head start on them, they wouldn't be able to catch him. . . .

Springing to his feet, he bolted out of the cabin.

Abner leapt from his chair, knocking it over, cursing the boy. While his sons dashed after Little Sun, who was heading across the meadow, running for all he was worth, their father bellowed, "After him! Hurry! Don't let him get away!"

Jake and Emmett flew out the doorway and off the porch in hot pursuit, while Abner stood on the edge of the porch, shouting encouragement to his sons. The shorter, stockier Jake could not keep up with his lanky younger brother, and soon Emmett was several strides ahead and widening the gap.

Straining every muscle, Little Sun made a beeline for the timber, knowing his chances of eluding the killers would be much greater amid the trees and shadows. He would find a hiding place, wait them out, then head for home.

He was within fifty yards of the forest when he heard Emmett coming on fast. He looked back to see his pursuer and stumbled over a rock that was sticking up out of the ground. Tumbling head over heels, Little Sun rolled to his feet quickly, but the few seconds of lost time was enough for Emmett to close in. The boy let out a wail as the young man seized him and hoisted him off the ground, then started back toward the cabin.

Little Sun kicked and screamed, attempting to free himself from Emmett's strong hands. Swearing, Emmett told him to settle down and shut up, but the boy fought with all his might. Just as they reached Jake, who was catching his breath, Little Sun slipped from Emmett's grasp and shot away, heading once again for the timber.

Emmett sprang after him, sank his fingers into the boy's buckskin shirt, and threw him violently to the ground, knocking the breath out of him. Cursing again, Emmett picked Little Sun up and slapped him across the face. Although the slap stung, the boy did not cry. Instead, desperate for his life, Little Sun tried again to run.

Furious, the lanky young man doubled up his fist and cracked Little Sun on the side of the head, and the boy fell to the ground, stunned. Emmett picked him up and hauled him back to the cabin, where his father commended him for retrieving the boy. Feeling proud of himself, Emmett stood Little Sun on the porch and cautioned, "Don't you try to run away again, kid! You hear me?"

The boy's head was clear once again. Tears glistened in his eyes as he spat back, "I *will*! I'll run away, and when my papa gets his hands on you, he'll beat you up good!"

"Oh, yeah?" Emmett crowed, grabbing hold of the boy's arm. "Well, your old man ain't gonna get the chance!" With that, he slapped and backhanded the boy several times, then let him drop to the porch floor.

Little Sun curled up into a ball, crying. Blood ran

from both nostrils, his upper lip was split, and angry red welts mottled his cheeks.

Standing over the boy, Abner said roughly, "I'm warnin' you, kid! You try to run away again, and I'll break both your legs! You got that?"

Little Sun knew the big ugly man meant what he said. Sitting up, he meekly nodded and wiped blood from his mouth, replying, "Yes, sir."

At midmorning, Abner stepped out on the porch and looked south across the meadow, eyeing an outcropping of rock that jutted forty feet from the meadow floor, near the timber. The rancher called to Jake, and when the young man stepped outside, his father pointed to the formation. "I want you to climb to the top of that rock," he told him. "It oughta be tall enough so's you can look over the trees. See if you can spot Reese comin'."

Obediently, Jake struck off across the meadow. Abner went back into the cabin and looked down at the battered Indian boy, who sat on the floor near the table. Grinning cruelly, he shook his head and said, "You really are a mess, kid. See what tryin' to run away got you?"

Little Sun looked at him coldly but did not reply.

Seated at the table, Emmett was carving his initials in its top with his pocketknife. Abner put a hand on his son's shoulder and said, "You did good, catchin' the brat and bringin' him back."

Emmett looked up, grinned, and said, "Thanks, Pa."

Squeezing the young man's shoulder, the patriarch said tenderly, "You know you're my favorite, don't you, boy?"

"Yeah, Pa," Emmett breathed. "I know."

Marshal Long Shadow had ridden for nearly twenty miles before he realized that the terrain was far different from that drawn by Reese Curry on the map, and he suddenly knew he had been sent on a wild goose chase.

Rage tore through him. Wheeling the horse around, he gouged its flanks with his spurs and raced furiously back toward Cheyenne Crossing. This time, if necessary, he would torture the truth out of Reese Curry.

Then his heart sank.

By the time he reached town, it would be almost noon . . . too late to save Little Sun's life. Reese no doubt figured his father would find another way to save him from the noose, and ensuring the death of Long Shadow's son was the killer's way of taking vengeance on the lawman.

Imagining the terrible death facing his child at Abner Curry's hands, Long Shadow was seized by a horrible panic that so constricted his throat, he could hardly breathe. When he thought of what Little Sun had to be going through at the moment, anguish ripped at his heart.

Then the anguish turned to hate. If that devil in human flesh took the life of his boy, the entire planet would not be large enough to hide Abner Curry. Long Shadow would find him. And when he did . . .

Sitting on the porch, Abner Curry watched Jake hurry across the meadow from the rock formation. He got to his feet and pulled a watch from his pocket. It was three minutes past twelve. *And by the look on Jake's face*, he told himself, *there's no sign of Reese*.

Jake stepped onto the porch and shook his head. "Ain't nothin' movin' out there, Pa. Looks like that stinkin' redskin didn't take you serious about killin' his kid."

Abner's response was a string of curses.

"So you gonna kill him now?" Jake asked hopefully.

Looking inside the cabin at the boy, whose face was stiff with fright, Abner scratched at his week-old beard and growled, "Not just yet. Maybe somethin' delayed 'em along the way. Let's have some lunch; then you go back to the rock and keep watch. We'll give 'em till an hour before sundown to show up. If they ain't here by then, the kid dies."

It was just past three o'clock when Jake Curry, sitting atop the towering rock and mopping sweat, caught sight of movement due south of his position. Shading his eyes and squinting, he was able to make out two riders coming his way.

Removing his hat and bending low so as not to be seen, he watched the riders as they intermittently passed from sunlight to shadow, threading their way through the forest. They were about thirty yards from the edge of the meadow when Jake recognized his brother on the lead horse. Reese was hatless and had his hands shackled. To Jake's surprise, the rider on the horse following was the Cheyenne wife of Long Shadow—holding a revolver aimed at Reese's back.

Sliding down the rock on its back side, Jake darted into the timber, circling so he could come up behind April Dawn and take her unawares.

Abner Curry was stretched out on a bed in the cabin's front bedroom, looking through the open doorway into the large room. He pulled out the pocket watch and saw that it was nearly three-thirty. Stuffing the watch back in his pocket, he called to his son, who was guarding the Indian boy in the next room. "Emmett!"

"Yeah, Pa?" the young man replied.

"Take a look out there and see if Jake is still up on the rock."

Abner waited, listening to his son's footsteps as he stepped out onto the porch. Ten seconds later, the footsteps became louder and Emmett appeared in the bedroom doorway. "He ain't up there on the rock, and I don't see him anywhere in the meadow."

Scowling, Abner grumbled, "Now, where the heck did he get to? Bring the brat in here so I can watch him while you go find your brother."

# Chapter Twelve

**W**hen April Dawn and Reese Curry neared the edge of the forest, they were some five hundred yards from the cabin. The killer said over his shoulder, "If you look a bit to your left, among those trees just beyond the far end of the meadow, you can see the place."

Looking past him, she could barely make out the roofline, since several clumps of trees, brush, and thicket stood between them and the cabin. Assessing the landscape, she told him, "We will ride through the meadow until we reach that large stand of brush and juniper trees. There we will rein in behind the vegetation and be sheltered from the cabin's view."

His head half turned, Reese asked, "Then what?"

There was a tremor in April Dawn's voice as she replied, "You will call out to your father and ask if my son is still alive."

"And if the answer is no?"

"You will die," she said simply.

The stocky young man swallowed hard. "If the answer is yes?"

"Then you will tell your father to come out of the cabin with Jake and Emmett. Their hands are to be empty and held over their heads in plain sight. They are to send Little Sun out ahead of them and do noth-

152

ing to endanger his safety. If they don't do as I order, I will blow your head off."

It was clear that Reese believed every word April Dawn uttered.

Jake Curry halted at the edge of the forest to the right of Reese and the Indian woman and watched them closely. Having circled around the pair, he was poised to dash up behind April Dawn, grab her gun hand, and throw her to the ground.

When April Dawn and Reese started slowly forward, Jake made his move. He sprinted from tree to tree as quietly as possible, getting within a few steps of her, when suddenly hoofbeats thundered behind him.

The Indian woman and her prisoner twisted around in their saddles in time to see Long Shadow fly from his lathered horse and slam into Jake. His impact was such that the two men rolled on the ground for several yards before coming to a stop. Drawing rein along with Reese, April Dawn kneed her horse closer to him and warned through clenched teeth, "There is no way you can outrun a bullet. If you try, you would not get ten feet."

Reese said nothing, keeping his gaze riveted on the two men.

Long Shadow gained his feet before Jake did and headed for him. His opponent then stood, yanking his gun out of its holster as he did so. But the lawman had by then gotten close enough to kick the weapon from Jake's hand, and it sailed into the grass, out of reach. Howling with pain, Jake lunged for the marshal, but he ran into a rock-hard fist with a great deal of muscle behind it. Long Shadow's punch caught him flush on the jaw, and he slammed to the ground on his back, the breath gushing out of him.

As Long Shadow went after him, Jake rolled over, leapt to his feet, and pulled his knife from its sheath.

Murder was in his eyes as he gripped the sharp weapon and screeched, "I'm gonna split you open and feed your guts to the birds, red man!"

Having spotted the cabin at the other end of the meadow and assuming it was occupied by Abner and Emmett, Long Shadow did not want to use his revolver and arouse them. He would have to take Jake another way.

Just then Jake, his knife aimed at Long Shadow's chest, lunged at the Indian, but the lawman lithely sidestepped the deadly blade and got in a couple of solid punches. Jake staggered back a few steps, then planted his feet and came after the marshal again.

While the combatants continued to fight it out, Emmett Curry was walking along the perimeter of the meadow in search of Jake. He spotted the figures just inside the tree line two hundred yards away. Quickly positioning himself for a clearer view, he made out the two riders on horseback and saw the fight going on nearby. No one had seen him, and—remaining carefully out of sight—he dashed closer. Hauling up behind a clump of brush, he focused on the riders, and his heart began beating hard when he recognized Reese, handcuffed and with April Dawn holding a gun on him. It took only seconds to identify the two grapplers.

Pulling his gun, Emmett ran toward the scene.

Long Shadow dodged Jake's deadly knife blade several more times, waiting for the right opportunity to seize his opponent's knife arm and rid him of the weapon. When the stocky young rancher swung the knife yet again, the Indian suddenly got his chance. Jake stumbled slightly, going off balance, and Long Shadow grasped his wrist with both hands and gave it a violent twist. Over the sound of the bone snapping, Jake screamed shrilly, and the knife slipped from his grip.

The marshal released the screaming man, but he soon found that he had underestimated him. There was still some fight left in Jake Curry. His right arm hanging limply, Jake stumbled toward where the knife lay on the ground. Snatching up the weapon with his left hand, he charged after Long Shadow, clearly determined to fight it out to the end.

The seasoned lawman knew it was kill or be killed. Avoiding the knife blade one more time, he leapt behind Jake, clamped his head in a fierce grip, and wrenched it unmercifully. Jake struggled, but his effort was fruitless against Long Shadow's strength. The young man's spine cracked with a sickening sound, and Jake fell dead with a broken neck.

Coming on the run through the meadow, Emmett was about sixty yards away when he saw his brother die. He immediately came to a halt, slipping on the grass. Reese spotted Emmett as his little brother pivoted and began running back toward the cabin, and he called Emmett's name at the top of his lungs. The youngest Curry stopped momentarily and looked back.

"Emmett!" Reese called again. "Is the Indian kid dead?"

Long Shadow and April Dawn looked over at Emmett and waited for his reply.

"No!" Emmett shouted, and he turned to run again.

Relief was immediately evident on the faces of Long Shadow and April Dawn, but then Reese abruptly shouted, "Tell Pa to kill the kid *now*! His old man just killed Jake!"

As Emmett again bounded for the cabin, Long Shadow screamed, "Emmett! If Abner kills Little Sun, Reese will die!"

Emmett did not slacken his pace. He ran as if the devil himself were after him.

Looking down at the marshal from the back of his horse, Reese cursed him and roared, "You're a lawman! You should have tried to take Jake alive! You didn't have to kill him!"

Long Shadow snapped harshly, "I *did* try! He wouldn't let me! I'll take *you* alive if your father will allow it. If not, I'll kill you, too!"

Stepping over to his wife, he asked her if she was all right. "I'm fine," she assured him. "Especially now that you're here and I know our son is still alive."

"We'll keep him that way," Long Shadow promised.

Turning away, he went over to Jake's body and removed the sheath from his belt. Picking up the knife, he jammed it into the sheath, then strapped it on his own belt. Then he rummaged in the grass until he found Jake's revolver. Putting it into his saddlebag, he pointed across the meadow and said, "Let's head for that stand of juniper trees up there."

April Dawn smiled. "That is exactly where I was heading when you showed up."

Minutes later they reached the spot. Leading his horse, Long Shadow dismounted, then helped his wife dismount. She eased the hammer down on the revolver but continued to clutch it as Reese was ordered from his horse and made to sit on the ground.

Peering through the thicket, Long Shadow studied the cabin. There was no movement. He turned and folded his beautiful Cheyenne wife into his arms and said comfortingly, "It's going to be all right, darling."

She leaned her forehead against his chest for a few seconds, then raised her face and asked, "Are you angry with me for taking things into my own hands?"

Shaking his head, he replied, "Of course not. You apparently knew that I had been sent on a wild goose chase and realized that the life of your son depended on this very action. No, far from being angry at you, I think you are most courageous."

Relieved, April Dawn put her head back on his chest. Long Shadow held her tight as he looked at Reese Curry, sitting nearby on the grass. Scowling, he told the killer jaggedly, "Your little trick almost worked, Reese. But I'm here, and I'm going to get my son back. And as soon as I do, I'm taking you back to Cheyenne Crossing so you can be hanged for murder."

Emmett Curry dashed into the cabin, his face white. His father was still lying on the bed, while Little Sun was sitting bolt upright on a chair, as if he was afraid to move a muscle. Abner sat up on the edge of the bed when his son came bolting through the door, and Emmett exclaimed breathlessly, "Pa! Long Shadow and his wife are out there in the meadow, and they have Reese with them!"

"Good!" Abner said, immediately standing and heading into the parlor. "Looks like he's ready to make a deal."

Emmett followed, hesitant to tell him the rest of it. Little Sun walked behind the young man, his face hopeful.

Abner had not yet reached the front door when his son mumbled, "I have to tell you somethin' else, Pa."

The rancher stopped short of the door and spun around. His eyes narrowing, he muttered, "I don't like the tone of your voice, son. Somethin' tells me what you've got to say is gonna be unpleasant."

"It is. When I got out there, Long Shadow and Jake were fightin'—and I saw Long Shadow kill him. He broke Jake's neck."

Abner paled. "You're sure?" he asked hoarsely.

"Yeah."

Hurling curses, Abner whipped the gun out of his

holster, thumbed back the hammer, and aimed it at
Little Sun. "I'm gonna kill this brat right now!" he
snarled.

"Wait a minute, Pa!" Emmett blurted, jumping in
front of the boy. "Don't do it!"

"Gads, boy! I could've shot you! Get out of the way
right now!" came the sharp command.

"Pa, no! You're not thinkin'! Long Shadow has Reese
out there in shackles. If you want to get him back alive,
you need the kid as a bargainin' tool. If he's dead, you
have nothin' to hold over that redskin's head."

His favorite son's words had a calming effect on Abner,
and after a few seconds he nodded slowly and said,
"You're right, boy. You're right. We've got to use the
kid to get Reese back. Once we do, *then* I'll kill him."

He sneered down at Little Sun, who stared back with
eyes huge with fright. The vein in the boy's temple was
pulsating rapidly, and little whimpering sounds came
involuntarily from his gaping mouth. Even though he
was a very brave child, the Currys' cruelty had by now
worn down his courage. He could see no way to escape,
and he prayed to the Great Spirit that Long Shadow
would soon rescue him.

Abner walked over to the kitchen area and pulled
open a couple of cupboard drawers before he found
what he was searching for. He pulled out a wad of
heavy twine and walked back to Emmett, instructing,
"Here. Take this and tie the kid to the chair to keep
him there. I'm gonna get Long Shadow's attention and
threaten to blow his kid's head off unless he frees Reese
at once."

The sun began to set over Devil's Tower to the west
as Abner appeared on the porch and shouted, "Long
Shadow! Can you hear me?"

Long Shadow and April Dawn exchanged glances

when Abner's voice sliced through the air. Parting the brush so he could see the cabin, the lawman called out, "I can hear you!"

There was a pause, and then Curry shouted, "Your kid's still alive. But if you don't give me my son, I'll kill yours! Let Reese go right now! I'm in no mood for games!"

Long Shadow wanted to be sure Little Sun was indeed alive. "I want to see my son, Curry!"

"He's okay. He's inside the cabin with Emmett!"

"*I want to see him!*"

Abner turned and said, "Emmett, bring the brat out here."

Holding the boy's arm securely, the young man ushered him out onto the porch, and Little Sun immediately screamed, "Papa! Mama! Help me! They're going to kill me!"

Before Long Shadow could say anything to his son, Emmett dragged him back inside and closed the door. The lawman looked down at his wife; she was doing her best to be stoic, but the tears spilled over her lids as she silently cried.

"You've seen your kid, Marshal!" came Abner's husky voice. "Now let Reese go! When I have him here with me, you'll get *your* boy!"

"No deal, Curry!" Long Shadow shouted. "Reese has been convicted of murder. He goes back with me!"

"Then why did you bring him here, if you didn't want to bargain?" the rancher yelled, his voice filled with confusion.

"I didn't plan it this way," the marshal replied. "It's a long story."

"Save your blasted story!" Abner roared. "Give me my son, or I'll kill yours!"

"Reese is going back to Cheyenne Crossing to hang!

If you kill Little Sun, you'll pay for it with your own life! You and Emmett are under arrest for kidnapping! Don't make it worse! Send my boy out to me, then follow with your hands in the air!"

Abner shouted back, "You already killed two of my sons, stinkin' savage! I owe you! I'm not gonna let Reese hang! Let him go, or your kid dies!"

April Dawn looked on fearfully. Gripping her husband's arm, she pleaded, "Long Shadow, you must let him have Reese, or he will kill our child!"

Reese nodded and stated, "You'd better listen to her, lawman. My pa means what he says."

Scowling, Long Shadow rasped, "You know full well your father has no intention of letting my son go, even if you are freed. I killed Bud and Jake. Abner will kill Little Sun for revenge." He put his hand on April Dawn's shoulder and said, "Somehow I must get in there and rescue him."

April Dawn sighed. "In my heart I know you are right," she concurred. Raising a shaky hand to her temple, she asked, "How are you going to do it?"

"I don't know yet. I need to think. It'll be dark soon—and that might give me the edge I need."

"What about it, Marshal?" Abner shouted, his voice echoing across the open meadow between them. "You want this kid dead?"

Long Shadow's eyes narrowed as he bellowed, "If you touch Little Sun, I'll kill Reese right here and now! Then *you* will die! And if I have to go through Emmett to get to you, he'll die, too! I mean it! Better think about that, Curry!"

Calling softly to his father from just inside the cabin door, Emmett urged, "Give him till sunup to let Reese go, Pa. I know that meadow like I know the back of my hand. I'll sneak out there when it's dark and kill that slimy redskin."

Abner turned to his son. "Forget it, Emmett. You wouldn't stand a chance against him. Besides, he's already killed two of your brothers. I won't give him the opportunity to harm you, too."

"You want to save Reese from hangin', don't you?"

"Of course."

"Then let me go out there after it gets dark. I'm tellin' you, Pa, I'll have the advantage over him in the dark. I can kill him. Then we'll have Reese back safe and sound, and we can hightail it outta these parts."

Abner thought over the idea. He had no better plan, and some kind of risk would have to be taken. "All right, son," he reluctantly agreed. Then, lifting his voice, he shouted, "Tell you what, Long Shadow! I'm a patient man! I believe if you have the night to think this situation over, you'll come to your senses! You have till sunrise to give me my son. If you don't, you've seen the last of yours. End of conversation!"

With that, Abner Curry entered the cabin and slammed the door.

Night settled in quickly, and the moon began rising. After gagging Reese, Long Shadow told April Dawn, "It's dark enough for me to be able to sneak up to the cabin. Once I'm there, I'll find a way to break in and surprise them. It wouldn't be the first time I've busted in on outlaws since I've worn this badge, and I'm sure I'll be successful this time, too. Little Sun will soon be in your arms."

April Dawn picked up Barry Hawkins's hair-triggered revolver and cocked it. Pointing it at the prisoner, she said, "I will watch this one closely while you are gone."

Smiling, her husband remarked, "You make a fine deputy, April Dawn. I will instruct you as I've instructed other deputies I've had: If he makes any kind of move toward you, shoot him. Even with his hands cuffed, he is dangerous. One move . . . kill him. Understand?"

The Cheyenne woman's face was grim. Flicking a hard glance at Reese, she answered, "I understand."

Squeezing his wife's shoulder, the lawman said softly, "I'll return soon."

Long Shadow sprinted across the meadow, angling toward the deeper shadows of the trees as he drew near the cabin. Reaching the trees, he circled around behind the weathered cabin and studied it for a moment. There was no way to look inside, for dark shades were pulled down on every window. Sporadic dots of yellow lantern light shone through tiny holes in the shades, but none of the holes was large enough to allow a view of the cabin's interior.

The marshal thought of the many outlaw hideouts he had stormed in the past. He had always employed the element of surprise by crashing through a door or window, gun blazing. But this time it was different. Inside this cabin was his only son. There was no room for error.

While he was at the rear of the cabin, contemplating the best avenue of attack, Long Shadow heard the front door squeak open. Hurrying around the side, he made his way to the front corner and flattened himself against the rough log wall, peering at the porch. Emmett Curry stood holding the knob and was saying over his shoulder, "Don't you worry none, Pa. Even though there's moonlight, I can do it. That scale-bellied Indian will soon be dead."

Emmett closed the door and stepped off the porch. Long Shadow's heart began pounding excitedly at the unexpected opportunity to get the younger Curry out of the way. He would hit him from behind and knock him out, then take him to where April Dawn waited with

Reese and make him explain the layout of the cabin's interior. If Long Shadow knew where they were keeping Little Sun and could lure Abner away from him, the rescue would be less dangerous.

The young man walked a few yards into the dark shadows thrown by the trees and stopped, squinting across the moonlit meadow and apparently planning his strategy. Moving silently behind him, Long Shadow brought the barrel of his Colt .45 down solidly on Emmett's head, mashing in the crown of his black Stetson, and Emmett Curry collapsed in a heap. Tossing Emmett's gun in some nearby bushes, the marshal hoisted the limp form over his shoulder and headed around the perimeter of the meadow, keeping to the tree line. When he was a safe distance from the cabin, he lay the young man down and used his own bandanna to gag him. Then he removed Emmett's belt and lashed his wrists behind his back. Picking Emmett up again, he continued on his course.

As the marshal slowly moved through the shadows it occurred to him that he now had Abner Curry's favorite son as his prisoner—and that gave him equal bargaining power. His hopes soared as he realized he might be able to get Little Sun freed without bloodshed.

# Chapter Thirteen

At the clump of trees and brush, Reese Curry sat on the ground off to April Dawn's side, trying to figure a way to overpower the Indian woman and escape before Long Shadow returned. He noticed that her gun was almost dangling in her hand rather than aimed at him, and it was apparent that her attention was focused far more intently on the cabin than on him. Suddenly Reese knew how he would get out of his predicament: He would use the same tactic his father was using and take the *woman* hostage. If he could take her unawares, she would not have the chance to use the gun on him.

Feeling that the worried mother was too engrossed in attempting to determine the outcome of her husband's mission to notice what he was up to, Reese silently scooted closer to her. Little by little, a few inches at a time, he neared her, getting ready to spring.

He finally did so, throwing his shackled hands over her head and locking the handcuff chain against her throat. Taken by surprise, April Dawn flung up her arms, and the gun sailed into the thicket.

Reese did not really need the gun; he had the best defense of all—April Dawn's body shielding his. Holding the struggling woman tight, one hand clamped over her mouth, he peered through the brush and saw the

dark form of Long Shadow coming toward them, carrying a large burden on his shoulder.

Abruptly the form flung over the lawman's shoulder
began regaining consciousness, grunting and kicking,
and Reese realized it was his brother Emmett. When
the marshal was about forty feet away, Reese pulled his
captive out from behind the thicket into the full light of
the moon. "Hold it right there, Indian!" the killer
shouted. "In case you can't see it, I've got this chain
pressed against your wife's dainty little throat. You do
what I tell you, or I'll strangle her!"

Halting in his tracks, Long Shadow felt the blood
drain from his face. "Let her go, Reese!" he commanded hotly.

"I'm callin' the shots, redskin!" Curry barked. "Let
Emmett down easy, then draw your gun with your
fingertips and let it drop."

Emmett grunted furiously against his gag and flailed
his feet. Long Shadow dropped him hard, slamming his
head against the ground. The force was enough to again
stun the young man.

"I said *easy*!" Reese snapped.

"Sorry, I guess I had it backwards," the Indian retorted mockingly. His right hand dangled near the butt
of his revolver, but he did nothing.

"The gun, lawman!" Reese shouted.

When the marshal still hesitated, Reese pulled the
chain tighter against April Dawn's throat until it
choked her. "Do as I say, red man, or I swear I'll kill
her!"

Fury boiled up inside the Cheyenne. With lightning
speed, he whipped out his gun, lining it on Reese's
face, which was partially hidden behind April Dawn's
head. Aiming his Colt directly at the killer's right eye,

he held his hand as steady as a rock and warned, "I said, let her go!"

Reese laughed wickedly. "Come on! Who do you think you're kiddin'? Nobody's that sure of his marksmanship, so you ain't gonna fire. It's too risky."

Through clenched teeth, Long Shadow hissed, "For the last time, Curry, let her go! I'm warning you!"

Swearing, Reese bore down harder.

The gun bucked in Long Shadow's steady hand, sending a slug through Reese's eye and out the back of his head. He fell to the ground, dead, taking April Dawn with him.

Long Shadow holstered his weapon and dashed to his wife. Freeing her from the dead man's hold and helping her to her feet, the tall Cheyenne said, "I'm sorry, sweetheart. I couldn't wait any longer. I had to shoot."

Coughing, she said haltingly, "I . . . wasn't worried. I've never known you . . . to miss your target."

Emmett was lying flat on his back a few feet away, rolling his head back and forth. Hurrying to him, Long Shadow knelt and searched Emmett for any hidden weapons. He quickly found the young man's derringer and slipped it into his own pocket.

April Dawn gestured at the younger Curry and asked, "How did you capture him?"

Before the lawman could answer, Abner Curry's voice roared out from the cabin. "Emmett, did you get him? I heard a shot!"

Whipping out his Colt and cocking it, the marshal jerked Emmett to his feet and pressed the muzzle to the base of the young man's skull. He then pulled off the gag and ordered, "Tell him you're my prisoner, nothing else!"

Abner called out again, worry evident in his voice. "Emmett? Can you hear me?"

"Go on!" Long Shadow commanded.

"I . . . I'm here, Pa!" Emmett shouted back.

"Go on! Tell him I have you in custody," the lawman directed.

"Did you kill him?" Abner pressed.

"No, Pa! He's got me in custody!" Then, before the lawman could stop him, he added, "The Indian killed Reese, Pa! Shot him through the head!"

Silence prevailed for a couple of seconds, and then it was shattered by Abner Curry's shrill cry of pained disbelief. Burning with fury, the rancher roared curses at Long Shadow, promising, "I'm gonna blow your kid's head off right now!"

The marshal shouted back, "If you do, I'll do the same to Emmett!"

"That's a rotten lie," Abner countered. "There's a badge on your chest, remember? You took an oath to uphold the law—and killin' Emmett in cold blood is against the law! But I ain't beholden to no stupid oath! Killin' a snot-nosed Indian brat won't bother me!"

"All I have to do is take off this badge, Curry, and I won't be obligated to my oath! You kill my son, and I'll blow Emmett's brains out . . . then I'm coming after *you*!"

Abner yelled, "You already killed three of my sons! And I believe in an eye for an eye!"

"Your sons are dead because you taught them to be greedy and heartless!" Long Shadow declared. "If any-body's responsible for their deaths, you are! You want to get even with the man who killed them, then put a gun to your own head and pull the trigger!"

"It's a dog-eat-dog world," Curry bellowed, "and I

taught my boys to go after what they want and take it before somebody else grabs it! So save your cock and bull!"

"You want to talk about saving something? How about saving Emmett? You've already lost three sons; you want to lose him, too? Your last son? And he's the special one, isn't he?"

"Yes, he is!" Abner shrieked. "You harm him and I'll—"

"No harm will come to him if you send Little Sun out here right now! Then you throw down your weapons and come out behind him! I'm warning you, Curry, don't push me. If you want to see Emmett again, do as I say!"

There was silence again.

Presently Abner called out, "I'll make you a deal! Free my boy right this minute! Once he's here in the cabin with me, I'll let your kid go!"

April Dawn touched her husband's arm. "Long Shadow, maybe he's telling you the truth!" she whispered, her voice catching. It was obvious that her need for hope overrode her good judgment.

"The man is lying, April Dawn!" her husband rejoined forcefully. "You heard him. He's only interested in getting even. He plans to kill Little Sun, no matter what happens. As much as it hurts me, I have to keep things as they are until I can trick him into making a mistake—which is the only way we'll get our son back."

Closing her eyes as if to block out the painful truth, the beautiful woman nodded.

Emmett snorted. "My pa ain't no dummy, lawman. He ain't gonna be easy to trick."

"That's my worry, not yours," the marshal growled.

"What *is* your worry is what's going to happen to you if your father harms my boy!"

Growing impatient for an answer, Abner shouted, "What about it, Marshal?"

"No deal!" Long Shadow snapped. "Give me my son right now!"

"You're not goin' to get your kid that way! Emmett must be freed first!"

"Then we've got us a deadlock, Curry!" Long Shadow yelled.

Swearing profusely, Abner whirled and stomped across the room. Little Sun was tied to a chair beside the table, and the rancher stood over him, breathing hard. Glaring at the boy, he snarled, "Your old man's a fool!"

Angered by the man's words, Little Sun retorted, "My father is not a fool! You're the fool!"

Enraged, Abner slapped him savagely across the face, causing the boy and his chair to topple over. "We'll just see about that, boy!"

Words were fired back and forth between the two fathers throughout the next day, but neither would give in. The sun began to set; the deadlock continued.

Long Shadow had paced all day like a caged bear. Periodically he would stop to make sure Emmett's handcuffs were secure and that the rope that now bound his ankles was tight; then he would resume his pacing. Now he paused in front of April Dawn, who sat on the ground holding Barry Hawkins's gun in her hand, and told her, "This can't go on. I'm going to just barge in there and rescue our boy!"

"Good idea, lawman!" Emmett scoffed as he tried unsuccessfully to find a comfortable position. "My pa'll be expectin' you to come, so he'll be ready to kill your son the second you go chargin' in there." The young man abruptly stopped speaking, and it was obvious that he felt he had said too much.

"He's right, Long Shadow," April Dawn said. "You can't take the chance."

Frustrated, the Indian turned and faced the cabin, barely visible in the deepening gloom of dusk, and shouted, "Curry, I'm running out of patience!"

"Then give me Emmett!" came the cold reply.

"No!" the marshal bellowed.

"Then we're still in a deadlock!" the rancher shouted.

Suddenly, her nerves shattered, April Dawn broke down and wept uncontrollably. Long Shadow knelt down beside her and tried to comfort her, but his preoccupation with finding a solution to the deadlock prevented him from doing little more than giving lip service. And his rage over the ordeal Abner Curry was putting his son through was reaching its flash point.

Abruptly releasing April Dawn, Long Shadow rose and glared at Emmett Curry, his hand going to the knife that he now wore on his belt. He pulled the weapon out of the sheath, and the razor-sharp blade glittered in the light of the rising moon as the lawman strode over to his captive.

Emmett looked up at Long Shadow, and he started at the sight of the knife. "Wh-what are you gonna do?" he stammered.

Without answering, the Indian pounced on Emmett, pinning him to the ground, and placed the tip of the blade against his Adam's apple, nicking the skin. Gasping, Emmett begged, "Don't kill me! Please don't kill me!"

"Don't worry, I won't kill you . . . yet. I need you. You're going to talk to your father and tell him that if

my son is not released soon, you're going to die
Indian-style . . . real slow! You'll experience such terrible agony that you'll beg for death to relieve you!"

Eyes bulging with horror, Emmett Curry choked,
"I-I'll try."

Long Shadow jerked him to his feet. "You're being
smart! Now, talk to him!"

The terror that Emmett felt was evident in his voice
as he cried out, "Pa! Pa! Don't let this go on any longer!
I think this redskin's goin' crazy! He'll kill me, Pa! He'll
torture me to death! Let the boy go! Please! I'm beggin'
you!"

Standing on the porch, Abner Curry listened closely
to his son's words and was affected by the genuine fear
in Emmett's voice. He nervously began to pace, pon-
dering the situation. He loved his son deeply, and
Emmett's anguish pained him. But he would not let
Little Sun go free. The boy was going to die as a
punishment to Long Shadow for killing Bud, Jake, and
Reese. However, he would make the Indian *think* he
was going to set the kid free.

Suddenly he had an idea. Glancing at the high-
powered Remington .44 rifle he had brought along,
Abner decided he would lure Long Shadow close to
the cabin, then take him out with a high-velocity
slug.

He turned and looked across the moonlit meadow to
the clump of brush. "Long Shadow!"

"I hear you!" The reply came sharp and clear.

"I've thought it over! Don't harm my boy! Let's break
this deadlock! At dawn, you bring Emmett up here to
the cabin, and we'll exchange sons face to face!"

Without a moment's hesitation, Long Shadow answered, "Dawn it is!"

Chuckling, Abner Curry entered the cabin, closing the door behind him. Stepping to the Indian lad still tied to the chair, he smiled smugly. "Like I told you, kid, your old man is a fool."

The rancher seized the back of Little Sun's chair and dragged it across the uneven wooden floor into the front bedroom, where a lantern burned on an old dresser. Placing the chair in line with the door, he then picked up a small table in a corner and set it down near the door in line with Little Sun's chair.

Going into the main room, he picked up the rest of the wad of thick twine that he had used to truss the boy with, plus the Remington .44 rifle. He worked the lever of the rifle to eject the high-powered cartridges, which he stuffed in his pocket, then returned to the bedroom. Smirking at the boy, he placed the rifle on the tabletop, aiming its ominous muzzle at Little Sun's chest.

A horrified expression on his face, the boy watched as Abner used the twine to anchor the rifle in place on the table. When it was secure, he ran another piece of twine over the trigger, then walked to the door. He made sure there was enough slack so that when he left the room, he would be able to reach in through the cracked door and loop the twine over the knob, thereby arming the trap. The gun would fire when the bedroom door was opened wide.

Rubbing his palms together gleefully, Curry laughed and said, "Now, Indian brat . . . let's see if it'll work."

Little Sun sweated profusely as Curry cocked the trigger on the empty rifle and prepared for a dry run. Exiting the room, the rancher swung the door almost shut, leaving just enough space to work his hand around the edge and slip the loop over the knob. The door then closed completely, leaving the terrified child alone, facing the rifle. After a few seconds, the knob turned and the door opened. The twine went taut, and the hammer came down on the empty chamber.

Abner guffawed. "Pretty smart, eh, boy? Works like a charm!"

He ran through the process one more time to make sure it was failure-proof, and then he checked Little Sun's bonds. He had previously bound the boy's arms and torso to the chair, and now he tied his ankles to the wooden legs.

Returning to the main room, he rummaged through the cupboard and drawers and found what he sought: several long nails. He then went outside and poked around the base of the cabin until he found a hefty rock; going back inside to Little Sun's bedroom, he used the rock as a makeshift hammer and nailed the four chair legs to the floor. Satisfied, he left the lantern to burn down and stretched out on the bed with his revolver in his hand, while the boy spent the night in the chair.

Neither of them slept. Just before dawn, Abner took a cartridge from his pocket, slipped it into the chamber of the rifle, and cocked it, making sure that the muzzle was still aimed straight at Little Sun's chest.

Using his bandanna, Curry gagged the boy. As he was tying it over Little Sun's mouth he explained, "I've got it all worked out, kid. When your old man brings Emmett, thinkin' we're gonna trade sons, I'm gonna put a bullet in that lawman's heart. Then I'll open that door and kill you. The reason I'm leavin' you alive for now is just in case your old man has some kind of trick up his sleeve, I'll still be able to bargain. Can't bargain if you ain't breathin'. And there's always the chance somethin' could go haywire, and I might take a bullet. Well, if that should happen, and your pa's still alive, *he'll* kill you when he opens the door. If I kill him but take a bullet, too, then your *ma* will kill you when *she* opens it." He laughed maliciously. "Looks like you lose, no matter what, wouldn't you say?"

The shades were still down on the windows of the bedroom as the husky man picked up the twine. Looking at the boy, he remarked, "Better say your prayers, kid—if you heathens say prayers. 'Cause next time that door opens, a bullet's gonna end your life." Without another word, he stepped through the doorway, set the trap, and closed the door tight.

# Chapter Fourteen

**B**reathing heavily with excitement, Abner Curry groped through the dark room, finding the corner where the other two rifles were leaning against the wall. It took only seconds for his fingers to identify the high-powered one, for it had a more intricate and sophisticated gunsight than Jake's—and that gunsight would enable him to get a bead on his quarry long before the lawman was in range to fire back.

Carrying the well-balanced weapon, the rancher felt his way to the front window, raised the thick shade, then opened the window and peered out. It was completely black, for the moon had dropped behind the trees, and no stars were visible. It was the darkest moment of the night, which meant dawn was only minutes away.

As he cradled the rifle in the crook of an arm, the heavyset man leaned against the window frame and whispered, "Won't be long now, stinkin' redskin! I've got one heckuva surprise for you!"

Ten more minutes brought the first gray light of dawn. Though the clump of trees and brush where Long Shadow waited with Emmett was not yet discernible, Curry peered in its direction. As the light grew stronger, he saw why he had not been able to see any stars: The broad sweep of the meadow was covered

with a ghostly fog, the result of warm air meeting with
cool ground. A slight breeze caused the fog to swirl as it
wafted over the meadow into the surrounding forest,
making the scene look as though it were under water.

Squinting again through the drifting vapors toward
the lawman's shelter, Abner could just make it out.
Lifting his voice, he shouted, "Long Shadow! You ready
to make the exchange?"

"Ready!" came the quick reply.

"Okay! Bring my son to me! When you're fifty feet
from the porch, I'll bring Little Sun out! This deadlock
will then be over!"

He quickly pulled the tattered old window shade
down to within a few inches of the sill. Dropping to his
knees, he laid the rifle across the sill, levered a cartridge into the chamber, and sighted down the barrel.
His pulse quickened when through the mists he saw
the two tall men emerge from the brush. As they drew
closer, he could see that the one wearing the buckskin
shirt and white hat was holding a revolver on Emmett
in his black hat and plaid shirt.

Abner's eager forefinger felt the smooth curve of the
trigger as he gripped the rifle, ready to fire. His eyes
glinted with an insane light, and his mouth curved into
an evil grin. The closer they came, the clearer was his
target. Sighting in on the white Stetson, he slowly
brought the gunsight down and leveled it dead center
on the buckskin shirt.

"That's right," the rancher whispered encouragingly,
his eyes straining to pierce the thin fog. "Just a little
closer, Indian, and you're a dead man!"

When the marshal and his hostage were less than a
hundred feet away, Abner felt a tightness creeping up
between his shoulder blades. Taking a deep breath, he
made sure of his aim and squeezed the trigger.

The rifle barked, sending its sharp report across the misty meadow. "I got him!" Abner shrieked triumphantly as the man in the buckskin shirt went down, a high-velocity slug in the middle of his chest. The rancher automatically jacked another cartridge into the rifle's chamber as he jumped to his feet, jerked the front door open, and ran out onto the porch.

Laughing ecstatically, he waved his free hand in a beckoning motion and cried, "Come on, Emmett! Come on! You're free now!" The man in the black hat came on the run as Abner continued gleefully, "That's it, son! Hurry up! We did it! That dirty redskin—"

Abner's breath caught in his throat and his scalp prickled. The face under the hat was not his son's . . . it was Long Shadow's! The lawman was raising the derringer in his right hand while reaching behind his back for the revolver under his belt. "Hold it right there, Curry!" the marshal bellowed.

It was more reflex than clear thinking that caused the beefy rancher to swiftly raise the rifle and fire. The derringer in Long Shadow's hand discharged, sending the slug into the air as he collapsed flat on his back and lay still.

Abner Curry stood frozen on the porch. His blunt face was a mask of stricken disbelief as he looked beyond the sprawled form of Long Shadow to the crumpled heap that had been his youngest son. Abner was a crack shot with his rifle. He had carefully aimed for the heart . . . and he knew he had hit his target. His voice rose in an ear-splitting screech as he railed at the fallen lawman, "You tricked me, you rotten scum! You tricked me! You made me kill Emmett! All my sons are dead now! I have nothin' to live for! I killed you, stinkin' Indian! Now I'm gonna kill your son!"

Wheeling, Abner dashed back into the cabin. Halfway to the bedroom door, overcome with grief, he threw his head back and screamed over and over, "Please, forgive me, Emmett! Oh, my son, my son! I didn't mean to kill you! He tricked me! I didn't know it was you! Please, forgive me, Emmett! . . ."

Sobbing, he stumbled to the closed bedroom door. Saliva spewed from his mouth as he raged, "Now it's your turn to die, Indian brat." Reaching out, he turned the doorknob and yanked the door open.

Inside the bedroom the rifle roared. Pivoting, Abner stumbled to the old table and leaned on it, tears flowing down his cheeks. His breath coming in labored sobs, the grieving rancher wailed insanely, "I killed my baby boy! I killed my baby boy! My own precious Emmett! I shot my baby boy!"

He looked down at the weapon in his hands, the one that had taken the life of his son, and knew what he had to do. Taking a live shell from his pocket, Curry jacked out the spent cartridge and loaded the high-powered rifle. He then turned it and stuck the barrel in his mouth, reached past the trigger guard, and pressed the trigger.

Racing across the meadow, April Dawn had reached her fallen husband and was kneeling beside him when the first shot rang out from the cabin, and the horrified woman's hand went to her mouth. Long Shadow had been right. Abner Curry had had no intention of releasing Little Sun and had planned to kill the lawman all along.

Her husband's plan had seemed a good one: Long Shadow had forced Emmett to exchange clothes, and as they walked toward the cabin, Emmett had held Jake's empty revolver on Long Shadow, while the lawman had the derringer concealed in his hand, aimed at Emmett's side. The hostage knew that he would get a .38-caliber slug if he tried to escape or called out a warning to his father. The only unknown was whether his father had set Long Shadow up for the kill—and Abner had done exactly what Long Shadow had figured he would.

April Dawn had been praying that her husband would have been able to fool the rancher just long enough to get the drop on him, but that had not been the case.

Screaming her son's name, April Dawn started to rise when her husband moaned, and she quickly dropped to her knees again. The black Stetson lay beside him, a rip in the crown where Abner's bullet had plowed through it. It had creased the lawman's temple, and the concussion of the high-velocity slug had knocked him out, but he was beginning to stir. There was a slight trickle of blood at the hairline.

Although she feared the worst for her son, she choked back her sobs and, breathing a prayer of thanks that her husband was alive and not seriously injured, she began ripping a length of her petticoat to serve as a bandage for his head. Suddenly Abner Curry's tortured wails came from the cabin, and her head jerked up. Then another rifle shot roared out, and all went quiet.

The marshal attempted to sit up. Shaking his head, he winced at the pain it brought and raised a hand to his bleeding temple.

Through her tears, April Dawn murmured, "Let me help you."

When he was sitting up, Long Shadow focused on her face. Then he turned his head sharply toward the cabin, wincing yet again, and asked in a tortured voice, "Did I hear a shot?"

Breaking down, April Dawn cried, "Yes. There were two of them. I fear that Curry has killed our son."

"We must find out," Long Shadow whispered hoarsely. He struggled to stand, and the gallant Cheyenne woman helped her husband to his feet. Cocking his revolver, he instructed, "You wait here. I'm going in there."

Staggering slightly, the lawman headed for the cabin. He climbed onto the porch and flattened himself against the wall beside the door, gun ready. April Dawn inched closer, watching him intently. After a few seconds, he spun around and kicked the door open, plunging inside.

Unable to just wait helplessly, the Indian woman picked up her skirt and ran toward the cabin. She leapt onto the porch but stopped short when she saw her husband standing just inside the door. Rushing beside him, she looked down and saw the body of Abner Curry on the floor with the top of his head blown away.

Sickened by the sight, April Dawn looked up at her husband. He was staring toward the partly open bedroom door, and she quivered as she took hold of his arm. They were both certain their son was in that room . . . and neither wanted to enter for fear of what they would find.

"Oh, Long Shadow," the frightened mother whimpered. "I . . . I can't bear to go in there."

Swallowing hard, the tall Cheyenne holstered the gun and breathed shakily. "Stay here. I'll go."

Just then they heard a muffled groan from the bedroom. Eyeing each other for a split second, they darted to the door. Long Shadow reached it a step ahead of his wife and pulled it wide open. A gaping hole had been punched through the window shade by the rifle bullet, which then had shattered the glass behind. And lying on the floor, tied to a fallen chair, was Little Sun.

Both parents hurried to him and immediately righted the chair. The relieved couple broke into sobs, embracing their son and showering him with kisses.

The boy's gag was removed, and while they untied him, Little Sun quickly explained the predicament Abner

Curry had left him in. He had figured that his only chance to live was to shift his chair out of the line of fire of the rifle trap, and though the legs of the chair had been nailed to the floor, the boy had felt a slight give in the old boards when he leaned from side to side. While the rancher was setting up to shoot Long Shadow, Little Sun worked the chair as quietly as he could. When the shooting started, followed by Abner's loud screaming, the boy rocked the chair hard until the nails worked loose. He had toppled it only seconds before Abner Curry had flung the door open, intending to kill him.

Once he was out of his bonds, Little Sun flung his arms around his parents, weeping for joy at a reunion he never expected to have. Long Shadow clutched his son to his chest, giving thanks to the Great Spirit for a happy ending to their ordeal.

The threesome filed outside to see that the fog was lifting, and sunlight streamed through the branches of the tall pines. In the distance to the west, the lofty summit of Devil's Tower seemed to be touched with gold.

Little Sun stood between his parents, holding their hands. He took a deep breath and said, "It's wonderful to be alive!"

Long Shadow laughed and said, "It certainly is! And there's a little girl waiting at Cheyenne Crossing who's wondering if any of us are alive. Let's go home."

Hand in hand, they stepped off the porch of the old cabin and headed across the meadow toward the horses.

## THE BADGE: BOOK 22
## GUN TRAP
### by Bill Reno

It is May 1864, and the feud between the Winnemucca and Young America mines in Aurora, Nevada, is heating up. When one of the mineowners hires Judd Colden and his gang of killers as strong arms, the violence that is already a daily fact of life in the rugged mining town escalates.

Determined to prevent an all-out war between the two factions, Sheriff Jess Packard, who has a well-deserved reputation for being tough on lawbreakers, is soon fighting battles on several fronts. Struggling to maintain peace in his town, Packard also gets caught up in more personal conflicts—ones that threaten his impending marriage, his relationship with his brother, and his career as a lawman.

Then tragedy strikes, and when the townspeople—his fiancée among them—denounce the lawman's integrity, he sets out to clear his name and polish away the tarnish clinging to his badge and his reputation. In the course of his pursuit, he finds happiness with a beautful young woman—but his future with her and his future as a lawman may well come to a violent end if he cannot escape from a deadly trap set by Judd Colden.

Read **GUN TRAP**, on sale April 1991, wherever Bantam paperbacks are sold.

**FROM THE PRODUCER OF WAGONS WEST
AND THE KENT FAMILY CHRONICLES—
A SWEEPING SAGA OF WAR AND HEROISM
AT THE BIRTH OF A NATION**

# THE WHITE INDIAN SERIES

This thrilling series tells the compelling story of America's birth against
the equally exciting adventures of an English child raised as a Seneca.

| | | | |
|---|---|---|---|
| ☐ | 24650 | White Indian #1 | $4.50 |
| ☐ | 25020 | The Renegade #2 | $4.50 |
| ☐ | 24751 | War Chief #3 | $3.95 |
| ☐ | 24476 | The Sachem #4 | $3.95 |
| ☐ | 25154 | Renno #5 | $4.50 |
| ☐ | 25039 | Tomahawk #6 | $4.50 |
| ☐ | 25589 | War Cry #7 | $3.95 |
| ☐ | 25202 | Ambush #8 | $3.95 |
| ☐ | 23986 | Seneca #9 | $3.95 |
| ☐ | 24492 | Cherokee #10 | $3.95 |
| ☐ | 24950 | Choctaw #11 | $3.95 |
| ☐ | 25353 | Seminole #12 | $3.95 |
| ☐ | 25868 | War Drums #13 | $3.95 |
| ☐ | 26206 | Apache #14 | $3.95 |
| ☐ | 27161 | Spirit Knife #15 | $4.50 |
| ☐ | 27264 | Manitou #16 | $4.50 |
| ☐ | 27841 | Seneca Warrior #17 | $3.95 |
| ☐ | 28285 | Father of Waters #18 | $4.50 |
| ☐ | 28474 | Fallen Timbers #19 | $4.50 |
| ☐ | 28805 | Sachem's Son #20 | $4.50 |